WICKED LIARS

WINDSOR ACADEMY BOOK ONE

LAURA LEE

WICKED LIARS ©2020 Laura Lee
SPECIAL EDITION COVER

∼

Editor: Ellie McLove of My Brother's Editor

Special Edition Cover Design: Books and Moods

prologue

JAZZ

It's funny the things you think of when you're dying. Like, I wonder what kind of birthday cake Ainsley got? I was hoping for chocolate, maybe with a raspberry filling... although, I suppose it doesn't matter anymore. Or... it'd be really cool if I was walking on the beach right now, feeling the ocean tickle my toes as the waves crash against the shore. I bet some local going out for a jog will find my body. Haven't you ever noticed that? Runners always find the dead bodies. I can see the headlines now:

Teenager Stabbed to Death in Quaint, Mountain Town

It'll shake up this community temporarily, but before you know it, I'll just be that poor girl who died by the water's edge. Goosebumps scatter across my flesh as a chill courses through my body. Damn, it's

1

cold up here. Of course, the one time I actually wear a dress, I get stuck out in the wilderness.

What really pisses me off—and yes, I have every right to be pissed as I lie here bleeding out—is that I can't stop thinking about the fact the people responsible for this will get away with it. They'll graduate high school, go off to college, eventually get married and pop out pretentious little babies, never looking back. Never knowing what it's like to have consequences for their actions. These people will always live in a world where you can solve any problem, get away with any vile act, by throwing a little money around.

My body sinks into the ground, the smell of mud and copper assaulting my senses. I really should get help, but moving isn't exactly an option. Screaming isn't one either—I've already tried that, and all I have to show for it is a raw throat. My head lolls to the side, eyes falling to the glassy surface of the lake as the fingers on my non-broken hand flutter over my abdomen, unsuccessfully trying to staunch the flow of sticky blood.

As I stare unblinkingly at the full moon reflecting off the lake's surface, I realize the irony of my situation. I'm no stranger to violence—I've spent most of my life surrounded by it. When you're impoverished, or craving your next fix, you'd be surprised what people will do when desperation sinks in. That's why my mother taught me to be vigilant, to take precautions. I took her lessons to heart and managed to survive over seventeen years without incident.

It fucking figures that when I actually *do* become a victim of violence, it's in a place drenched in wealth.

I suppose that's what I get for trusting a liar.

chapter one

JAZZ

"Here we are." My social worker, Davina, shifts her rusty old Ford Focus into park.

I stare out the windshield at the sprawling mansion before me. "Wow, you weren't shitting me when you said he was rich, huh?"

Davina's brown eyes light up in amusement. "You might want to watch the language around your father, Jazz."

"Don't call him that," I snap.

She gives me a sympathetic look. "Honey, I know this is hard, but—"

I scoff. "You think?"

Davina is undeterred by my interruption. "Jazz. Listen. I know you miss your mom. Any girl in your situation would. But I'd hate to see you screw up an opportunity like this because you have something against rich people."

"I don't have anything against rich people," I argue. "I have something against a man who can obviously afford child support but would rather pretend his kid didn't exist."

"Who said he was pretending?" she challenges. "He claims he genuinely had no knowledge of your existence until your mother approached him shortly before her death."

I shake my head. "I don't believe it. Whenever I asked my mom about him, she was always so cryptic. She said he wasn't a good man, that we were better off without him, and that's all I needed to know. Why in the hell would she go to him after almost eighteen years? Why didn't he ask to meet me *right away* when she did supposedly inform him that he has a kid?"

"Jazz, I can't speak for your mom, but I can assure you we checked him out." Davina sighs. "He's an upstanding citizen and successful businessman. Philanthropic, even. He didn't hesitate for one second when we contacted him. Charles Callahan is offering to give you a better life than anything you've ever known. You'll have opportunities you've never had before. If you don't care about yourself, think about your sister and how much you could improve her life with access to resources like this."

"Just because we were poor doesn't mean we had a

bad life. I always felt like anything would be okay as long as we had each other."

She gestures to the giant house in front of us. "I know that, honey, and I respect it. Your mom was a rock star for making the best out of a crappy situation. But she's gone and you and I both know your sister is not in the most ideal place right now."

Damn it. She's right. My seven-year-old sister, Belle, and I have different fathers. Hers has been in and out of her life since birth. He only seemed interested in being a parent when it was convenient for him. He agreed to take full custody of Belle when the state contacted him though and with their limited funding, they practically threw her at him.

He may not have a criminal record, but the man can't hold down a job to save his life and he's a raging alcoholic. Davina knows I want to fight for at least partial custody when I become a legal adult, so I can have a bigger say in how she's raised.

The problem with that is, realistically, no judge will just hand over a child to an eighteen-year-old with no home or job. Plus, there's bound to be exorbitant legal expenses that I need to consider. Whatever it takes, however long it takes, I'm going to make it happen. I know without a doubt, my mom would want this.

I squeeze my eyes shut briefly to ward off the tears. God, will this overwhelming sadness ever wane? It's only been a month since my mom died but it hurts just as bad—if not worse—than it did when that police officer showed up at my door. There's this constant weight on my chest that makes it hard to breathe.

Davina pats my shoulder. "I know it'll be an adjustment, but you'll be okay in time. We haven't known each other long, but I know you're strong and you're smart. You can get really far in life on those two things alone." Davina nods to the front door. "Now, go on. They're waiting for you."

"Why couldn't he pick me up from the group home? You know that's not giving him any brownie points, right?"

"Sweetie, we've been through this. Your father is out of town on business, but he's scheduled to return tonight. The house manager is there to welcome you on his behalf." As if on cue, the wooden double doors open and a woman wearing a black dress with her hair in a severe bun steps out onto the covered porch. "There she is now."

The house manager. That's right. What the hell does a house manager do anyway? I get out of the car, pulling my duffle bag from the back seat. Before I shut the door, I lean down to say goodbye. "Wish me luck."

Davina smiles. "I don't think you'll need it, honey, but good luck. You know where to find me if you need anything."

I step back and close the door. "See ya."

I watch as Davina pulls through the circular driveway before heading back the way we came. A throat clearing draws my attention away from the black car fading in the distance.

"Miss Jasmine, I'll take that bag for you."

I hitch my duffle higher on my shoulder and turn around to address the woman. "Please call me Jazz, and no thank you. I can carry it just fine."

Deep wrinkles form around her mouth as she frowns. "If you insist. Please, follow me, Miss Jasmine. We've been expecting you."

"It's *Jazz*," I mumble, irritated she so blatantly ignored my request.

It's painfully obvious how out of my element I am the second I step foot onto the polished golden floors. A double staircase stands before me, attached to a wide balcony with intricately carved iron balusters. The ceilings are the highest I've ever seen and the furniture is sparse but expensive looking. I look down at my worn denim and second-hand Chucks. The contrast between them and the marble beneath my feet is laughable.

"Right this way," the woman says, interrupting my musings.

I follow her up the stairs and down a seemingly endless corridor to the right. I briefly wonder if I should be leaving a trail of breadcrumbs in case I need to make a quick exit.

"Your room is right do—"

"What's your name?" I ask.

She gives me a stern look over her shoulder before

continuing her trek to wherever we're going. "You may call me Ms. Williams."

"And what do you do here, Ms. Williams?"

We finally—*finally*—stop at a door near the end of the hallway.

Ms. Williams turns the knob and steps aside, gesturing for me to enter. "I'm the house manager. I ensure everything is running smoothly according to Mr. Callahan's specifications."

Vague much?

I resist the urge to roll my eyes. "What exactly does that mean?"

She gives me a haughty look. "You'll learn soon enough, young lady. For now, let's just say that all staff members report to me. They are my eyes and ears around the estate. *Nothing* happens without my knowledge, which I then report to Mr. Callahan."

Message received loud and clear.

There are spies everywhere.

If I had to guess, I'd say my sperm donor is a control freak.

Ms. Williams clears her throat. "Now, as I was saying, this area of the house is reserved for you and Miss Peyton. You each have a bedroom with a built-in ensuite, then a shared game room—which also doubles as a small theater room—and a guest bathroom. I'll take you on a formal tour after dinner and you can see the rest. You'll have free rein over all common areas and guest rooms, but you are *not* permitted to enter the north wing unless invited. That's where Mr. and Mrs. Callahan reside."

Jesus Christ, who needs their own personal *wing*? This damn bedroom alone is bigger than my old apartment.

"Who the hell is Peyton?"

The wrinkles around her eyes and mouth deepen when she frowns. "Young lady, foul language will *not* be tolerated. It makes you sound like a hoodlum—I suggest you correct that immediately."

Oh, bitch, you just wait and see how much of a *hoodlum* I can be.

She continues, completely ignoring my glare. "As for Miss Peyton... she is your stepsister."

Wait a second... I have a stepsister? Why didn't Davina tell me that?

"How old is she?"

"She's seventeen, just like you. You'll both be starting your senior year at Windsor Academy the day after tomorrow."

"Wait... *what?*"

She ignores my question. "Your father will answer all of your questions at dinner—six o'clock sharp. Now, I have other matters to attend to. I suggest you freshen up and dress in something more *appropriate*." Ms. Williams looks me over from head to toe. "You're a Callahan now. You're expected to look and act like one. But don't worry; you'll find that your closet is fully stocked, so you'll have plenty of garments to choose from." She waves her hand in a circle. "A stylist is coming tomorrow morning to take care of that awful hair."

With that, she turns on her heels and leaves the room.

"What's wrong with my hair?" I yell as she closes the door behind her.

Who the hell does that woman think she is? What gives her the right to speak to me like that? I finger a lock of my long, dark hair, watching as the purple streaks shine in the sun. I *love* my hair. My mom loved my hair—she said it fit my personality. Why would I want to change it?

I'm doing this for Belle, I remind myself. I sigh and decide that I might as well explore a little while I'm stuck here. First up is the closet, which is as ginormous and as ridiculous as I'd expected. Hundreds of items hang from the rack with a wall of shoes that must cost more than my mom made in a year. In the center of the room, there's a built-in dresser filled with neatly folded jeans, pajamas, and frilly lingerie. Holy shit, can you say stalker? Not that I don't appreciate pretty things, but the fact that whoever bought this stuff knew all my sizes, down to my 34-B cup boobs, creeps me out.

"So, you're the charity case," a snooty voice says from behind me.

I startle before turning around to find a preppy-looking girl glaring at me. She's pretty—*really pretty*—and about my age. Her waist-length hair is so blonde, it's almost white, in stark contrast with her overly spray-tanned skin. She's dressed in a khaki skirt that hits mid-thigh with a light pink cardigan set and an honest-to-God set of pearls. As I'm taking her in, I see her lips curl in disgust as she does the same to me. This must be my new stepsister.

I fold my arms over my chest. "Ever hear of a thing called knocking?"

She does the same, pushing up her giant tits. Jeez, those suckers have to be fake. She's tiny, other than the overinflated balloons hanging off her chest.

"I *did* knock. You didn't answer."

I lift my eyebrows. "Yet you decided to invite yourself in anyway? What do you want, Peyton?"

Her glossy pink lips turn up in the corners. "I see you've heard of me."

"Unfortunately. Your bitchy reputation precedes you."

I know that was a bit harsh considering I just met her, but I've always considered myself a good judge of character. This chick is the textbook definition of a mean girl.

Her blue eyes narrow as she flips her hair over her shoulder. "Good. Your life will be much easier if you understand how things work around here."

I prop a hand on my hip. "Oh, yeah? What specifically are you referring to?"

Peyton straightens her shoulders and lifts her chin. "That you're only here because Daddy didn't want to tarnish his image by having a bastard child floating around. I'm his *real* daughter, in every way that matters. And when we get to Windsor, this is *my* year to rule. You'll keep your ghetto ass out of my way and you'll stay *far* away from my boyfriend, Kingston Davenport."

I smirk. "Insecure much?"

She scoffs. "Hardly."

"Then why are you warning me to stay away from your boyfriend?" I stick out my lower lip. "Aw, honey, are you *threatened* by me?"

Peyton curls her fists. "Listen, trash. You have *nothing* on me. Kingston wouldn't touch you even if his life depended on it. Sure, Bentley might let you suck him off—because let's face it, he'd let practically *anyone* suck his dick—but the minute he blew his load, he'd toss you to the side, because you're beneath us. *You don't belong.* The faster you get that through your tiny little brain, the better. Trust me when I say you *don't* want to fuck with me."

I smile, wondering what Daddy Dearest would think if he heard his little princess going off about blow jobs and dropping F-bombs. And who the fuck is this Bentley guy? My expression must make Peyton nervous because she starts shifting on her feet.

"No, *you* listen." She retreats with every step I take forward. "I grew up in the projects, bitch. Ever hear of a thing called street smarts? You can't imagine the things I've seen or what I've learned how to do. The

14

unsavory people I know. If anyone should be worried around here, it's *you*."

I've learned how to defend myself when necessary, but I'm bluffing for the most part. I've lived my life trying to avoid trouble whenever possible, but Peyton doesn't need to know that. I have a feeling if I don't stand my ground with this chick from the start, she'll trample all over me.

I fight the urge to cover my ears when she stomps her foot and lets out a shrill scream. "Just stay away from me."

Her long hair slaps me in the face as she turns and marches out my door.

"Gladly," I mutter.

Wow. Welcome to the family, Jazz.

∾

I manage to find the dining room right before the clock turns six. I may be early, but I'm still the last one to arrive. I'm also the only one who doesn't look like they're attending a posh luncheon at a country club. I didn't bother changing my clothes which I suspected would push the control freak's buttons.

If I'm being honest with myself, I'm actually excited about getting to wear the stuff in my closet, but this—a faded tank and cut-offs—is the real me. I want to make sure that my first impression on these people is as authentic as it gets. I recognize Charles Callahan from our one brief encounter as soon as I walk into the room.

He eyes me with distaste. "Jasmine, did Ms. Williams not show you where your new wardrobe is located?"

I take a seat at the far end of the fancy table. "Oh, she did, but I didn't feel like changing."

The woman sitting next to my father flashes a fake smile. Based on her major Stepford vibes, I'm guessing she's the wife. "I'm Madeline, dear. Welcome to the family."

"Uh... thanks." I nod to the basket of rolls sitting in front of her. "Pass the bread, will ya?"

My wicked stepsister snickers. "You might want to think about skipping the carbs. We wouldn't want any rumors floating around school that you're pregnant with some gangbanger's kid, now would we?"

Madeline chuckles. "Oh, Peyton, stop joking around, dear. Jasmine might think you're seriously trying to hurt her feelings."

Peyton presses her flattened palm over her heart. "I would *never* do such a thing, Mother."

Yeah, right.

Peyton gives me a look that clearly says she *is* trying to hurt my feelings. Too bad for her, I'm not taking the bait. I jump out of the chair and grab a roll before sitting back down.

Chewing through a big bite, I say, "It's all good. If

some vapid bitch wants to start a rumor about me, let her. I don't give a fuck what other people say."

I give Peyton a look that says *she's* the vapid bitch I'm referring to.

My stepmother gasps while my father says, "Cursing *will not* be tolerated in my home, Jasmine. I realize your upbringing has been subpar at best, but I will not allow any daughter of mine to sound so uneducated. It's unbecoming for a young lady to speak such filthy words."

I snort indelicately, earning a horrified look from his wife. "First of all, I prefer *Jazz*, not Jasmine. Secondly, my *upbringing* was just fine. You do realize this isn't the 1950s, right? Women swear all the time. I've even read a study recently that said people who curse often are typically smarter than those who don't."

His lips tighten as he waves a hand dismissively. "Regardless of what some study says, you are *Jasmine Callahan* now. There are certain expectations that come with our family name. Behaving like a well-educated and proper lady is one of them."

"Well, it's a good thing my last name is Rivera then, isn't it?"

Sperm Donor gives me a smarmy smile. "Not for long. I've expedited the name change process. The judge should sign off on it by the end of the week."

My jaw drops. "Excuse me? You can't just change my name."

His bushy eyebrows rise. "But I can, and I *will*. Until

you're a legal adult, the law says otherwise. Take it as the gift that it is, Jasmine. Being a Callahan will afford you certain privileges."

I cross my arms over my chest. "I never asked to be a Callahan and I don't need any privileges that come with it."

He narrows his icy blue eyes. "Stop being such a foolish little girl. You'll learn to appreciate it soon enough. Once you and your sister get to school, you'll need our family name behind you."

Peyton sneers. "Daddy is right, Jasmine. You'd be eaten alive at Windsor if you showed up as... *yourself*."

I give her a look that says, *I can handle myself, remember?*

I sigh. "What's the deal with this Windsor place? Based on the uniforms hanging in my closet, I'm guessing it's some kind of private school for rich assholes. Am I close?"

My stepmother places her hand over Sperm Donor's forearm when his face reddens. "Jasmine, dear, Windsor is an *elite* prep school. Anyone who graduates from there is practically a shoo-in for the Ivy Leagues."

I consider that for a moment. I've always dreamed of going to UCLA but never thought it'd be possible, despite the fact that I've maintained a 4.0 GPA. I could only imagine how many doors would open for my sister and me if I had a degree under my belt from such a reputable university. It's not an Ivy, but it definitely carries prestige. The last time I checked, their admissions rate was less than fifteen percent.

"Where is it?" These two seem like the type to ship their kids off to boarding school and the one thing I won't do is leave L.A. I need to keep an eye on Belle.

She takes a sip of wine. "We're quite fortunate that it's local—only about ten miles from here. You'll love it there—it's a beautiful facility. Only students from the upper echelon of society are admitted. It's an *honor* to be accepted. You're really fortunate things happened when they did—they *never* accept students after the first trimester begins, no matter how generous a donation may be. Your father had to pull some strings to get you enrolled so last minute."

I stiffen. "I'm *fortunate* things happened when they did?" I couldn't care less that I'm shouting right now. "What *things* are you referring to exactly? My mother's *death*?"

"Well... yes," she sputters.

Is this bitch serious right now? I'd give anything to be sitting on the couch with Belle and my mom, eating a bowl of Ramen for dinner instead of being at this monstrous table with a gourmet meal.

I fly out of my seat so fast, it topples over. "Fuck. You."

Peyton and her mother gasp as Charles shoots out of his chair and yells, "Jasmine! Apologize to your mother this instant!"

I point to the uptight blonde before me. "*She* is not

my mother." I move over to the younger version of her. "And *she* is not my sister." I nod to him. "As for you... we may share DNA, but I don't need a daddy either—I've gone my entire life without one and I've been just fine. And how many times do I have to fucking tell you people, call me *Jazz!*"

His face is so red, it's turning purple. "Go to your room right now, you disrespectful little shit!"

So much for the no cursing rule. Maybe that only applies to people without dicks.

I scoff. "Gladly."

I'm angry with myself for losing control, but I saw red when Madeline talked about how *convenient* my mother's death was. I know I'll need to suck it up for Belle's sake and be on my best behavior but I need some time to cool down first. The last thing I see before stomping up the stairs is Peyton's smug smile, telling me she's enjoying every minute of my misery. I'm definitely going to have to watch out for that one.

chapter two

JAZZ

The next morning is filled with one primping session after another. It seems Madeline Callahan has made it her personal mission to make me look like a proper young lady. The house manager woke me up at the crack of dawn, commanded me to shower, then led me down to the salon where my new stepmother and a team of stylists were waiting to pounce. Yes, there's an actual *salon* in this house, complete with adjustable height chairs, washbowls, nail stations, the works.

Madeline says the salon is an "absolute necessity" because a lady must *never* go out in public without looking her best. I swear the woman thinks we're Kardashians or something. Shit, I wouldn't be surprised if she knew them considering they live around here somewhere. I indulged her this time because I'm trying to be flexible for Belle's sake, but the bitch is crazy if she thinks I'm going to get up early every day to have my hair and makeup professionally done.

First of all, I have *no* desire to stick out and that'd be rather difficult if I looked as if I just stepped off a catwalk. Secondly, restful sleep is a rarity for me these days. I need every spare moment I can get if I actually manage to shut my brain down long enough to doze off.

My hair is now fully brunette—not a trace of purple, which Madeline says is against Windsor's dress code—and perfectly blown out. My skin has been waxed, exfoliated, and moisturized to the extreme, and the nails on my hands and feet are painted a glossy pale pink. Madeline practically had an aneurysm when I asked the tech if she had any black polish. Apparently, a *proper lady* only wears shades of nude unless there's a special occasion. Then, and *only* then, are reds acceptable. Under *no* circumstances, am I permitted to wear anything else because it would make me look *cheap*.

Cue the eye roll.

I already miss my mom with a gut-wrenching intensity, but this superficial bullshit amplifies it. Mahalia Rivera was the most beautiful woman I've ever known and she rarely wore makeup. Our Filipino heritage gave her skin a year-round bronzed look with eyes and hair the color of dark chocolate. She was incredibly fit from being on her feet all day working various jobs, and her smile could light up a room.

Her physical beauty wasn't where it stopped though. My mom had the biggest heart, always helping others no matter how busy or exhausted she was. She worked hard, sometimes three jobs at a time, but not once had she complained. My sister and I never doubted her love for us; it radiated from her. She proved it, day in and day out, with her actions. If more people were like her, this world would have a lot fewer problems.

I rub the aching spot on my chest. I've read that emotional pain from losing someone important to you is so paramount it can manifest into physical pain. I never quite understood how that was possible, but I definitely get it now. Ever since my mom died, the sharp pains in my chest and the pit in my stomach have been constant reminders she's no longer here. Sometimes it feels like my heart is literally splitting in two.

I take a deep breath before stepping out the back doors for inspection. Charles, Madeline, and Peyton are all sitting at a large table on the patio eating brunch. I guess they weren't worried about starting without me.

Madeline gasps. "Oh, honey, you look beautiful! Doesn't she look stunning, darling?"

Sperm Donor looks me over with careful scrutiny. "Yes, this will be... acceptable. For now."

What the hell? I just had to deal with people fussing all over me for *six hours* to bring me up to his standards. "What's the matter? I'm not blonde enough for you?"

All three members of my newfound *family* look Scandinavian, with pale hair and blue eyes. Even though Peyton is technically his stepdaughter, she looks more like Charles' birth child than I ever will.

His jaw tics. "Are you accusing me of something, Jasmine?"

I lift a shoulder in response.

A smarmy smile stretches across his face. "My first wife—God rest her soul—was Venezuelan and my second wife is African American."

Jesus, how many times has this guy been married?

"And?"

He dabs at the corner of his mouth with a napkin. "Not to mention the fact that your mother was Asian American. I certainly hope you're not implying I would have an issue with people of color because I think my history with women would contradict that statement. It's not a matter of race; it's about *class*. You may be wearing designer clothing and appear more refined on the surface, but you wear your lack of decorum like a badge of honor.

"I realize you grew up in a different socioeconomic environment so I'll give you some leeway, but you *will* learn how to carry yourself properly. If you can't figure out how to do that on your own, I'll have to sign you up for etiquette classes."

Peyton smirks. I scratch the bridge of my nose with my middle finger in response.

Charles narrows his eyes. *"That* only reinforces my statement."

I nod. "Got it. So, you're not a racist but you *are* a classist."

God, what is it about this man that compels me to run my mouth?

His face gets that purplish tint to it that I'm becoming awfully familiar with. "Classes begin tomorrow. I suggest you take the rest of the day to familiarize yourself with the Windsor Academy handbook. Their expectations of the student body are clearly laid out and *will* be adhered to."

I pop an eyebrow. "Or else?"

Madeline places her hand on his forearm, in attempt to diffuse the situation. "Dear, I'll have one of the maids bring some snacks to your bedroom. You just let them know if you need anything else."

I give a flippant wave as I step back inside. It's probably for the best so I don't say anything else that pisses him off. My self-control is obviously lacking where Charles Callahan is concerned. I have no desire to be around a man who can dismiss me so easily anyway.

∼

I'll admit, Windsor Academy's campus is impressive. I can't believe this place is right outside of L.A. It seems like a completely different world. As the town car pulls through the wrought-iron gates—of course Charles Callahan couldn't be bothered to drive me here—I'm dumbstruck by the beauty of it. There are three red brick buildings, with two stories each, lined up in a semi-circle. Smaller buildings are scattered throughout, all with a similar architecture. The grounds are meticulously landscaped and surrounded by thick woods comprised of mature evergreens.

I wipe my sweaty palms on my plaid skirt, reminding myself that I have no reason to be nervous. As the car comes to a halt, I see Peyton and two other girls standing next to a red sports car. The student parking lot is freshly paved and filled with ridiculously flashy vehicles just like it.

By the way the two girls are fawning over Peyton with plastic smiles, I'm guessing this is her mean girl brigade. Unlike me, Peyton has her license, so she drove herself to school. I resist the urge to roll my eyes as I step out of the car.

The stunning copper-haired girl to Peyton's left eyes me curiously. "Who's that?"

"Nobody," Peyton sneers. "Literally *nobody*. Forget you ever saw her."

All three girls giggle as I meet my driver, Frank, at the rear of the town car. I still can't get over the fact that I have my own personal driver.

He pulls my new designer leather backpack out of

the trunk. "I'll escort you to the administration's office, Miss Callahan."

"Frank, really, I can handle it. Just point me in the right direction and I'm good."

He eyes me skeptically. "Are you sure? Mr. Callahan would not be pleased if you got lost and were late."

I wink. "I can handle it."

Frank smiles sheepishly and looks back at Peyton. "I don't know. If Miss Devereaux—"

"Miss Devereaux is too busy with her adoring fans to notice. Really, Frank. I'm good."

He hands my bag over. "Very well. Good luck, Miss Callahan."

"Jazz," I correct.

He gives me a soft smile and points to the building in front of us. "Good luck, Jazz. The administration office is in Lincoln Hall, the center building. The office will be immediately to your right and they're expecting you. I'll be here to pick you up after school."

"Thanks. I have a feeling I'm going to need it. Have a nice drive back."

He nods. "Thank you, miss."

As I walk across the parking lot, I can feel people staring. I make a conscious effort to hold my head high, reminding myself that I give zero fucks what these spoiled brats think of me.

I finally make it through the crowd of students and breathe a sigh of relief as I ascend the steps into

Lincoln Hall. That is until I see three sets of eyes, standing off to the side, tracking my every move.

Damn.

I normally wouldn't look twice at a preppy douchebag, but these three wear their school uniforms *well*. I stumble when I lock gazes with the boy in the middle. Scratch that. There's nothing boyish about any of these guys. All three of them are tall, broad, and muscular. Jesus, what are their parents feeding them? Middle guy's icy stare causes all sorts of crazy, dirty images to run through my mind, forcing shivers down my spine.

Whoa.

I know it's cliché, but I've always had a weakness for bad boys and these guys are the epitome of one. Stupid teenage hormones.

I shake it off and make my way into the building which is an odd experience in itself. Even my elementary school had metal detectors and bag check stations before entering. I guess they don't think rich kids have a propensity for going postal. My eyes widen as I get my first glimpse of my new stomping grounds. Cherry wood paneling lines the walls with polished white marble flooring. There's no tiny metal graffiti-adorned lockers for these kids either; instead, they have full-sized wooden ones that are only a shade darker than the paneling. The whole place screams money. I swear it even *smells* like money.

My fellow students are openly gawking, looking at

me like I'm some sort of freak show. Geez, the social hierarchy in this place is painfully obvious, as if we're living smack dab in the middle of a teen movie. I shove that thought aside as I spot a sign indicating the office is just off to the right like Frank said. As I step over the threshold, I'm surprised at how opulent it is, although I suppose I shouldn't be considering it matches the rest of the place. There are several sturdy cherry wood desks in the middle of the room, each complete with state of the art computers and tiny decorative stained-glass lamps. There's a single door on the right wall with a brass nameplate indicating it belongs to the headmaster.

A frail woman wearing a black pantsuit barely takes her eyes away from her computer long enough to acknowledge me. "May I help you?"

"Hi... um... I'm new. I was told to come here first."

The woman raises her delicate silver eyebrow. "Name?"

"Jazz Rivera." I fidget as her fingers fly along the keyboard. "You might have me listed under Jasmine."

"I don't have a Jazz or Jasmine Rivera." She shakes her head. "I do, however, have a Jasmine *Callahan* who's scheduled to arrive today."

I bite my tongue, reminding myself that it's not her fault my sperm donor is an asshole. "Yeah, that's me. Although, my last name is legally Rivera." For a few more days anyway. "Could you please fix that?"

She finally meets my eyes, curiosity pouring out of

her. "I'm sorry, dear, but your father listed you as Jasmine Callahan on the registration forms. Only he can make any changes, so I suggest you check with him."

"That won't be necessary," I mutter.

The woman—Mrs. Stanford, according to her nameplate—hands me a tri-fold brochure. "Here's a map of the campus. You can find one stored on your academy issued tablet as well. If you'll take a seat, your buddy should be here any moment."

My eyebrows furrow in confusion. "Buddy?"

Mrs. Stanford sighs, as if I'm exasperating her. "Yes, Miss Callahan. Your *buddy*. All new students at Windsor Academy have one. It looks as if you're paired with Ainsley Davenport. She'll show you around campus and ensure you have all necessary course materials."

Why does that last name sound so familiar?

"I heard my name. This must be the noob."

I turn toward the cheery, feminine voice to find a beautiful brown-haired girl about my age, sporting a big smile which I can't help but return. She's the only person besides Frank who's shown me any sort of warmth since I stepped into this world.

She sticks out her hand. "I'm Ainsley and I'm guessing you're Jasmine."

I shake her hand. "I prefer, Jazz, actually."

Ainsley nods. "Jazz... I like it. It makes you sound badass."

"Miss Davenport!" the secretary scolds. "There's no need to use such crass language."

Ainsley rolls her eyes and nods toward the exit. "Let's get this show on the road, shall we?"

I smirk. "Lead the way."

As soon as we leave the office, Ainsley starts peppering me with questions. "So, what's your deal, new girl? How'd you end up in rich kid prison? Rumor has it you're Peyton Devereux's sister. Is that true?"

"*Step*sister," I correct.

Ainsley's eyes twinkle in amusement. "I'm sure that's... interesting."

"I just met her two days ago but so far, she hasn't left the best impression."

She laughs. "Yeah, don't hold your breath waiting for that to happen. Peyton's a stone cold bitch."

"So you know her?"

She nods. "*Everyone* knows Peyton Devereux. She makes sure of it."

"Sounds about right," I mumble.

"First stop is the library so we can get your Chromebook. All of your course materials will be on that. That's also where we'll get your student ID."

"Everything's electronic? What about books?"

She shakes her head as she pushes the door open to head back outside. "Yeah, right. Do you think these overprivileged brats would carry around heavy books all day?"

My lips twitch. "I'm going to go out on a limb and say that you don't like many people."

"That's not true." I'm caught off guard when she loops her arm through mine, but I decide to go with it. "I just don't like assholes and Windsor is filled with them."

I laugh, immediately deciding I like this girl. "Good to know. So, I should probably watch my back then, huh?"

"You should *definitely* watch your back. Everyone seems to have a motive and nobody cares who they have to step on to get what they want." She eyes me thoughtfully. "I hope you don't have any major skeletons in your closet. I wouldn't be surprised if some of these jerks have already run background checks on you to find blackmail material."

"*What?*" My jaw drops. "Are you being serious? Why would anyone even know I exist?"

"You're fresh meat—we don't get new students very often. Most of us have known each other since kindergarten, or even before. You're hot too, so just a heads up, most of the guys will probably try to fuck you—the straight ones anyway—and any chicks who want to fuck *them* will hate you. Not like they weren't catty bitches already, though. This school has a serious overabundance of them." Ainsley's cheeks pinken as she gives me a sad smile. "I have a bit of a confession. I already knew your story before we met—I was just asking to make conversation. I'm sorry about your mom, by the way. Mine died when I was eight, so I know how bad it sucks."

Her admission causes me to suck in a deep breath, but I don't get the chance to say anything before we're interrupted.

"Ainsley," a growly voice calls, causing us to stop. "A moment."

"Oh, boy, here we go," she mutters.

I look in the direction of the voice and come face to face with the three hot guys from earlier. Holy shit, they're even better looking up close. I quickly glance around and see all eyes on us. I'd bet anything these three are at the top of the food chain around here. They not only have that air of superiority, but the way the other students seem to cower down to them speaks volumes. It's not just their unmistakable physical dominance—these guys have that ineffable factor that demands attention. Their intense stares make the hairs on the back of my neck stand up.

Ainsley stops in front of the middle guy. "What do you want? I'm busy."

Well, I guess not *everyone* cowers down to them. It only makes me like Ainsley more.

"What are you doing, Ains? They pay people to take out the trash." He glares at me as he speaks to her.

Oh, no he didn't.

My adrenaline is flaring as I level him with a matching glare. "What's your problem?"

The dickhead completely ignores me and continues

talking to Ainsley. "Are you going to answer my question?"

Ainsley rolls her eyes. "Back off, Kingston. You may be two minutes older, but you're not the boss of me."

Wait... what? They're twins? Is this the guy Peyton was talking about? It has to be—that name isn't very common.

Kingston's stupidly square jaw tics as the guy on the right looks like he's trying not to laugh. "There are *rules*, Ainsley."

I'm about to hand this guy's ass to him, but Ainsley beats me to it.

She pokes him in the chest. "I can hang out with whoever I want and Jazz here, is my girl, so we'll be spending lots of time together. If you have a problem with that, too bad."

His jaw tics. "No. You. *Won't.*"

I throw my hands up, officially fed up with his bull-shit. "Seriously, what *the fuck* is your problem? You don't know me. *How dare you* make assumptions about me!"

His gold-flecked eyes—I'm now noticing are identical to his sister's—hone in on me. "That's where you're wrong, *Jasmine Callahan*. I know everything I need to know about you. And I suggest you keep your mouth shut or I will make your life a living hell."

I park a hand on my hip. "It's *Rivera*, asshole, so you obviously don't know *everything* about me. And if you think your threats are going to intimidate me, think again. My life is *already* a living hell."

He actually looks taken aback by that, but he masks it within seconds and focuses his attention back on his twin. "We'll discuss this later."

Ainsley scoffs and grabs my arm to lead me away. "Don't hold your breath."

I have to practically run to keep pace with her, all the while I can feel Kingston's wrath from behind us. "What the hell was that? That asshat is your *brother*?"

She stops in front of one of the outbuildings and steps to the side. "Yes. And believe it or not, he's not usually that bad. Don't get me wrong; he's an asshole by nature, but not usually *that much* of an asshole. It must be you."

I shake my head. "Lucky me."

Ainsley sighs. "Just ignore him. He's probably on his man period or something."

I laugh, grateful for the break in tension. "Let's hope. So... first up, library?"

Ainsley smiles and nods. "First up, library."

chapter three

JAZZ

My assigned buddy and I didn't have any morning classes together, so we agreed to meet up at lunch. My jaw drops when I step foot into the dining hall because it is not your average high school cafeteria. It's more like an upscale restaurant. Round tables that seat eight apiece are scattered throughout the cavernous space, each adorned with crisp white tablecloths.

I don't see Ainsley yet, so I head over to the buffet set up against the walls. According to my handbook, lunches are included in tuition so thankfully, I don't need to worry about scraping up money I don't have to pay for it.

"Miss." A man wearing a white coat hands a tray to me with a plate, cloth napkin, silverware, and a glass on it already.

"Thank you."

I check out the selection, which has several different types of soups and salads along with an assortment of dishes from around the world. Italian, Mexican, Asian, American—you name it, it's probably here. I choose some teriyaki chicken with steamed rice and an iced tea.

Tray in hand, I scan the room and finally spot Ainsley. *Oh, hell no.* There's an empty seat right next to her, but you couldn't pay me to sit at *that* table. Three of the chairs are taken by her brother and the other two guys he hangs out with. My wicked stepsister and her cronies occupy the other three. I spot an empty table across the room and make a beeline for it. I have no choice but to pass them on my way, so I keep my head down, hoping Ainsley doesn't notice me.

"Jazz, where are you going?"

No such luck.

"Hey." I jerk my head to the corner table in the back. "I think I'm just going to sit over there."

Ainsley gives me a sad smile as she takes in the six pairs of eyes drilling holes through me. Thankfully, she gets the hint, grabs her tray, and stands. "May I join you?"

I smile tentatively. "Sure."

"Ainsley," her brother growls. "I thought we settled this."

Of course it wouldn't be easy.

My new friend scoffs. "Oh, screw you, Kingston.

The only thing I *settled* on was the fact that you can't tell me what to do."

His hazel eyes narrow. "I'm looking out for you. Who knows what kind of diseases she's carrying?"

I fight the urge to punch this asshole in the throat. "Excuse me? First of all, *she* is right here, so if you have something to say, you can say it directly to me. Secondly, if anyone around here is riddled with *disease*, it's probably *you*. I hear chlamydia is on the rise—you might want to get checked out."

The mean girls let out a collective gasp. This little showdown has drawn the attention of everyone else in the room. They're gawking openly—not even trying to hide their interest. Geez, these people need to get a life.

"Oh, I *like* her." The gorgeous boy with the darker features winks. He's a mixture of ethnicities like me, but I can't quite tell which. Maybe African American and Asian? Possibly Pacific Islander. "The feisty ones are always freaks in bed."

I'm no stranger to crude teenage boys, so his attempt to shock me doesn't work. "Too bad you'll never know."

His thick veiny forearm flexes as he rubs a hand over his mouth. "We'll see about that, sweetheart. I'm Bentley, by the way. Just so you know whose name you'll be screaming out later."

Before I have a chance to retort, Kingston slams his fist on the table. "Shut the fuck up, Bent."

Bentley shrugs. "Hey man, don't be a cockblocker. She's hot."

What is it with these douchebags talking about me like I'm not in the room?

I make direct eye contact with Kingston. "I'm done wasting my time on this bullshit. Do me a favor and just stay the hell away from me and I'd be *more than happy* to do the same."

With that, I turn on my heels and walk away with Ainsley hot on my trail. Out of the corner of my eye, I see Kingston start to rise, but he stops when Peyton pulls on his arm and starts whispering something in his ear.

Ainsley laughs as she sets her tray down and pulls out a chair at our table. "That was awesome, Jazz. I haven't seen someone put my brother in his place in... well, *ever*. Besides me, that is."

I scoff as I take a seat. "Yeah, well, then I'd say it's long overdue. I can't believe you two are related."

"He isn't so bad once you get to know him. Believe it or not, Kingston actually has a heart deep down. Your sister and her plastic groupies are much worse— I'm pretty sure they sold their souls to Satan in exchange for lip injections and boob jobs."

"*Step*sister." I laugh. "She and Kingston definitely seem like the perfect match."

"Ha! Peyton wishes."

"What does that mean?" I take a bite of my food. Damn, this is good. Definitely not the cardboard pizza lunches I'm used to. I feel like I've entered an alternate universe.

"Kingston barely tolerates Peyton most days."

I tilt my head to the side. "But they're dating?"

She shrugs. "Sort of, but it's more about appearances than anything. They're the reigning king and queen this year. People expect them to be together. They were a real couple but they had a big blowout during the middle of junior year and he dumped her. She somehow convinced him to take her back over the summer, but it hasn't been the same. As far as I know, they pretend to be a couple in public and she turns her head to whatever he's doing in private."

My face scrunches. "What a pig. I can't believe Peyton puts up with that."

Ainsley takes a bite from her salad. "Don't feel sorry for her. She knows exactly what she signed up for. Besides, she's an untrustworthy cunt."

I smirk. "Wow, tell me how you really feel."

"Don't pretend like you don't agree." She grins as she looks over my shoulder. "I'm pretty sure she's not your biggest fan either. She hasn't stopped glaring at you since we walked away."

"Fuck her." I can feel the heat of her stare, but I refuse to acknowledge it. "What's the deal with the whole 'reigning king and queen' thing?"

"Every year, the graduating seniors pass the torch to three guys and three girls who pretty much rule the school. They've been groomed for it since freshman year, although if you ask me, not a single one of them needed help learning how to be an asshole. The other students treat them like royalty, hence the nicknames. Hell, even the teachers won't do shit to them because of who their parents are. This year, that's Kingston, Reed Prescott, and Bentley Fitzgerald for the guys and Peyton, Imogen Abernathy, and Whitney Alcott for the girls."

Jesus. Even their names are pretentious.

"And let me guess... for the rest of us, our choices are to kiss their asses or pay the price?"

"Pretty much. Although anyone who's chosen the latter usually doesn't stick around for long."

"Where do you fit in?"

"I guess you could say I'm next in line for the throne, although if they ever tried to promote me, I'd abdicate the shit out of it. I have no desire to be one of them. Everyone at Windsor knows who I am and nobody messes with me for the simple fact that I'm a Davenport, but I honestly wouldn't call any of these people my friend." She points to me. "I have a feeling you're the exception to the rule, though. We've known each other less than a day, Jazz, but I can tell you're different. What you see is what you get."

"I have no reason to hide anything. I'm not ashamed of who I am or where I come from. If anyone has a problem with it, screw 'em."

She waves her hand dismissively. "Enough about those jerks. How's your first official day been so far?"

I shrug. "Okay, I guess. I can already tell the coursework will be much harder than my old school but I'm following along easily enough."

"I can't believe we don't have any classes together until last period." Ainsley pouts as she reviews my schedule.

"Yeah, but it's not like we can change it, right?" I shrug.

"True." Her eyes widen. "Oh, shit."

"What?" I motion for her to pass my phone back to me.

Ainsley winces. "I'm pretty sure my brother is in your next class."

I reopen the Windsor Academy app and pull up my schedule. "AP Lit with Henderson?"

She takes a long sip of sparkling water before answering. "Yep. It's not like I have his schedule memorized, but I'm almost positive he's in that one."

Against my own volition, my eyes seek out said brother across the room. He's been staring directly at me for at least the last ten minutes, but I've been making a studious effort to ignore him.

"Great." I stretch the word out. I take another bite of my chicken.

"Damn, girl, keep that up and I might consider switching teams."

I finish chewing before replying. "Huh?"

"You just moaned. *Loudly*." She laughs as she glances

over my shoulder again. "Bentley looks like he just creamed his pants."

I look back, and sure enough, Bentley is watching me with undisguised hunger. My entire body flushes as my eyes roam to Kingston. It feels like there's an invisible tether between us, crackling with electricity. I've never felt anything like it before. He looks like he wants to devour me, but he also looks extremely pissed off about that. As much as I hate to admit it, my body reacts. Ugh, I really need to get a handle on these hormones.

I turn back around and take a deep breath. "There's not a chance in hell they'll just let me be, is there?"

Ainsley shakes her head. "Not likely. Prepare yourself, Jazz, because I have a feeling things are about to get *really* interesting around here."

chapter four

KINGSTON

That girl is going to be trouble.

When I first heard Charles Callahan's lovechild was coming to live with them, I didn't think twice about it. Knowing her mom just died, I assumed she'd be some meek, broken little girl who'd fall in line without question. Instead, she's this fierce, *stunning* creature, who seems far too observant for my liking.

I've been working on this project for too long to have a wrench thrown in my plan now. No matter how hard the new girl makes my dick, I cannot let that dick rule my actions. I've been putting up with Peyton for years trying to integrate myself into that family. She and I may have an agreement that I can fuck whoever I choose, but it goes without saying her new stepsister is the exception to that. Anyone with half a brain can see how threatened Peyton is by her, and I need to keep

49

Peyton in line to keep up pretenses. I'm so close to uncovering the evidence I need to ruin Charles Callahan. There's no way I'm going to let some piece of ass destroy everything.

"God, she's such a waste of space," Peyton whines. "Daddy doesn't even want her living with us. It's so obvious. I really wish he would've just let her stay in the system. She *so* doesn't belong."

Imogen, one of Peyton's minions, pouts. "You poor thing. I can't imagine living with someone so... uncouth. Did you hear the way she talks? And what's the deal with the red lipstick in the middle of the day? Like, oh my God, ghetto much? She looks like a whore."

"I certainly wouldn't say no to having that lipstick smeared all over my cock," Bentley quips.

I flash him a glare, but the asshole just smirks at me. Bentley and Reed are like brothers to me. We're so in sync, we can often read each other's minds. I'm sure Bentley knows my thoughts are currently echoing his.

Whitney, Bent's on-again, off-again fuck, scowls. "Gross. It's not even funny to joke about something like that."

His grin widens. "Who said I was joking?"

Whitney's lip quivers. "Baby, stop. People are going to think you're serious."

I have to fight the urge to plug my ears. I swear to Christ, that chick must have a mouth like a Hoover for Bentley to put up with her nasally voice.

"Oh-em-gee, you should've seen her before my mom's stylists fixed her hair." Peyton leans forward, smiling as if she has some juicy gossip. "She had bright purple highlights, split ends for days, and the rattiest clothes I've ever seen. I was totally embarrassed to be living in the same house with someone so trashy. Can you believe she refused to let them do her hair and makeup before school today? I'm pretty sure she's only wearing that slutty lipstick right now... *maybe* some mascara. And her hair is totally air dried! Can you imagine?"

I resist the urge to roll my eyes when Imogen and Whitney gasp. God forbid someone doesn't put on twenty layers of makeup and styling products in the morning.

Peyton laughs mockingly. "I guess you can take the girl out of the projects, but the projects will most certainly never leave *that* girl."

My eyes automatically follow said girl across the dining room. She's facing away from me, but as I take in her waist-length dark hair, I find myself imagining what it would look like with a pop of color. Hot as hell, I'm guessing. Bentley meets my eyes again and I can tell he's having the same thoughts.

Don't even think about it, my eyes warn.

If you're not going to tap that, I sure as shit am, his eyes reply.

I scowl, which only makes the asshole laugh.

"What's so funny, babe?" Whitney trails her nails

down his forearm, using the most obnoxious baby voice.

"Nothing, babe," he assures her. "Just guy stuff."

She pouts, clearly not satisfied with that answer but smart enough not to press for more. Well, look at that: you can teach a dumb dog new tricks.

Reed leans back in his chair and taps my shoulder. "She gonna be a problem, man?"

Reed's a man of few words, but his intuition is on point. He and Bent know my plan for destroying Charles Callahan. He can sense that Jasmine's arrival is something to be concerned about.

"Later," I tell him.

He nods, knowing this isn't the time or place for this discussion. I'm going to need a minute to figure out what our next move will be. The only thing I do know right now is that Charles' bastard will *not* fuck this up for me. If that means I have to fuck *her* life up in the process, so be it. Collateral damage is always inevitable in war anyway.

chapter five

JAZZ

I breathe a sigh of relief when I walk into AP Lit and see no sign of Kingston Davenport. I stopped by the bathroom on the way from lunch, so the class is pretty full by the time I arrive. The only open seats are in the last row, so I make my way down the aisle.

"Whore," one girl mutters as she makes a failed attempt to trip me.

"How much do you charge for blowies, honey?" This comes from some future politician looking douche who's eying me like I'm a big, juicy steak.

I ignore the derogatory whispers and stares, refusing to give them the satisfaction. Karma will bite these motherfuckers in the ass one day. Hopefully sooner rather than later. I keep my head down, pull my tablet out of my bag, and open the online classroom portal, waiting for our teacher to begin.

I glance up when all hushed voices suddenly stop. I assumed the teacher was approaching the podium, indicating the start of class, but I should've known better. Not only does Kingston walk through the doors right as the bell is ringing, but he's flanked by both Reed *and* Bentley. And, of course the only available seats are the three in my row.

Fuck my life.

Bentley flashes an arrogant smirk and drops his ass on the seat to my left. Kingston takes the desk beside him while Reed is on my right. I stare straight ahead, willing the damn teacher to start class already.

Hot breath hits my ear right before he speaks. "Hey, Little Red Ride Me From the Hood. Look at you, surrounded by three big, bad wolves."

Wily fucker. The wolves are Windsor's mascot and Bentley's obviously dogging where I came from. Too bad for him, I'm not ashamed of my roots.

I swat him away with my hand. "Clever. Now back the fuck off."

His chair protests as he scoots his desk closer. "You kiss your boyfriend with that mouth, *Jazzy Jazz?*"

I glare at him through the side of my eye. "Don't have a boyfriend, *Get Bent.*"

"Ooh, she has claws!" he taunts. "You know I love it when you talk dirty, baby." Bentley grabs his crotch. "Makes my dick *so* hard. Why don't you come a little closer and see for yourself?"

I eye his crotch and give him the most unimpressed

look I can manage. "Sorry, I forgot my microscope. How ever will I find it without one?"

Reed releases a deep chuckle. Well, I'll be damned. I made the silent, broody one react.

Bentley's jaw drops. "You apologize to him right now!" He looks down to his lap. "It's okay, buddy, she didn't mean it."

I try disguising my laugh with a scoff. Damn it, why do I find this idiot so charming?

"Don't hold your breath. Actually... I take that back. Please *do* hold your breath. If I'm lucky, you'll pass out and I won't have to listen to your ridiculous nonsense."

"Miss Callahan, is there something you'd like to share with the class?"

I glance up at the front of the classroom to find Ms. Henderson staring at me expectantly, her annoyance obvious. What the hell? I'm not the only one talking!

She raises a delicate silver brow. "Well?"

"No, ma'am," I mutter.

Ms. Henderson gives a tight nod. "Good. Now, keep quiet, please. Ladies and gentlemen, I hope you're comfortable because the seat you chose today will be yours for the rest of the trimester."

I stifle a groan.

When our teacher turns to write something on the whiteboard, Bentley leans over again. "Ooh, it looks like we're about to get some real quality time together, princess. Today must be my lucky day."

I grind my teeth together. "Shut. Up."

"Maybe I will if you give me that pretty red mouth of yours. I bet your throat feels *real nice and warm* on the inside. I've been thinking about it all day."

I fight a smile, wondering what Madeline would do if she saw me right now. She was already in a huff because I refused to let anyone do my hair or makeup this morning. Little did she know, I stashed my favorite mascara and lip stain in my bag and applied it during the ride to school. My uniform skirt is black and red plaid and the reds matched perfectly so I considered it a sign.

Bentley flips the back of my hair. "This silky hair of yours would look even better wrapped around my fist."

I'm about to tell this asshat to fuck off but the one next to him speaks up first.

"That's enough," Kingston growls.

Bentley slouches back in his chair. "Just having a little fun, man."

I glance over and see Kingston giving his friend a murderous glare. When his steely eyes flicker to mine, my breathing stops. Naked rage wars with lust, a heady combination that calls to me in the most primitive way. Shivers race down my spine when Kingston drops his gaze to my mouth and licks his lips. Something unspoken passes between us before a wicked grin forms on his face.

"Don't worry, Bent. There will be plenty of time for *fun* later."

What the hell does that mean? And why did my

mind automatically go to the gutter thinking of all the possibilities? I really need to get a handle on my attraction to him.

For the next forty minutes, I do my best to ignore the three ridiculously hot assholes next to me. The moment the bell rings, I dart out of the room as fast as possible.

As I'm crossing the threshold, I swear one of them says, "You can run, but you can't hide, princess."

~

Madeline is waiting for me right inside the front door when I get home from school. She scowls when she sees my red lips but that quickly morphs into a plastic smile.

"How was your first day at school, dear?"

I shrug. "It could've been worse. I met a really cool girl, so that's a plus."

"That's great! What's her name?"

"Ainsley Davenport."

Madeline's smile is genuine now. "Oh, that's wonderful! Ainsley is a lovely girl. Her mother and I are friends."

I frown in confusion. "She said her mother passed away."

"Oh, her birth mother did, quite a few years ago. I was referring to her stepmother, Vanessa. She's the third Mrs. Davenport." Madeline holds her index finger up. "Wait... the fourth. Or... maybe she's the third wife and he's her fourth husband? It's all so confusing."

"Of course," I say mockingly.

"You should get cleaned up and ready for dinner." She appraises me. "Please don't test your father's patience tonight and wear something nice from your closet. And remove that wretched color from your lips. The Davenports will actually be our guests for dinner. Unfortunately, Ainsley can't make it because she has ballet rehearsal, but her twin brother will be here. Have you met Kingston yet? He's Peyton's boyfriend."

You've got to be kidding me.

"Oh, I've met him. He's a peach."

My sarcasm either went over her head or she's choosing to ignore it.

"Fabulous!" Madeline clasps her hands together. "Dinner will be at six o'clock sharp. If you'll excuse me, I need to make sure the chef has everything I've asked him to prepare."

How is this my life? I groan as I head to my room, trying to think of a viable excuse to skip dinner.

chapter six

KINGSTON

"Would you like a scotch, son?"

I bite my tongue to prevent myself from lashing out. I'll never get what I need if Charles Callahan suspects how I really feel about him.

"That'd be nice, Mr. Callahan. Thank you for offering."

"How many times do I have to tell you to call me Charles, boy? We're practically family. Marrying Peyton is just a formality."

I'd like to say that will never happen, but if I don't manage to dig up his deepest, darkest secrets before then, it might. Peyton is a lot of things, but patient is not one of them. She's made it clear she expects a ring on her finger by Christmas and she has no intention of having a long engagement. She knows I'm using her, and the manipulative bitch is twisting it to her advantage. Peyton doesn't really care about me, but she *does* care about her image and the marriage clause in her trust fund. It's the only reason she agreed to this little arrangement of ours.

I pretend to be her doting boyfriend in public and she gushes about how wonderful I am to Daddy Dearest. Peyton thinks I'm trying to earn her dad's trust and respect so he'll make me partner in his firm once I graduate law school. The fact that she actually believes that garbage proves she doesn't know me at all.

I take the tumbler from him. "Thank you, *Charles*."

He laughs. "Now, was that so hard?"

My father laughs. "How are things at the firm?"

"Can't complain," Charles replies. "Our second quarter revenue was at a record high."

Yeah, I bet. Charles Callahan is one of the most successful criminal attorneys in the country. He has a perfect winning record so of course, anyone facing a nasty charge would want to retain him. It doesn't matter what you're accused of or how guilty you are. If you're wealthy enough, and Charles agrees to represent you, an acquittal is almost guaranteed. The man has so many officials in his pocket, it's obscene.

If my suspicions are correct, he has some pretty hefty blackmail on those officials from his business with my father. Neither one of them are aware I know about their disgusting side venture. It's one of the many cards I'm holding close until the timing is right. I need to play the game until I can gather enough evidence, no dirty judge or DA can dig them out of it. Hence, why I'm currently in Charles Callahan's cigar room, acting like I enjoy hanging out with these old pricks.

I grind my molars when he pats me on the back. "I've got some new Cubans for after dinner. You interested?"

"Of course he's interested," my father answers on my behalf. "What else would he do? Gossip with the hens?"

Both men laugh at that while I fight the urge to roll my eyes. I hate my father just as much as I hate Callahan. They're both narcissistic sociopaths and massive chauvinists. A woman's purpose in their world is to look pretty, keep their mouths shut and their legs open whenever they feel like busting a nut. I like fucking hot girls as much as the next guy, but women with nothing between their ears drive me insane. Sadly, there's not many options outside of our circle.

That said, nothing would make my father happier than watching me follow in his path, so I allow him to believe I share his opinion. And nothing would make Charles happier than pawning his daughter off to someone as wealthy as well-bred as I am. I wonder if he would still feel that way if he knew how many times I beat off earlier to fantasies of his *other* daughter.

"How are things going with Jasmine?" my dad asks Charles as he takes a seat on the tufted leather couch.

Well, now here's a topic I'll actually be interested in. It's like he read my mind.

Charles sighs. "Not well, Preston. Not well at all. She's stubborn, impulsive, and... rough around the edges. It's going to take *a lot* of effort to make her heel. Madeline has taken her on as a little pet project, so I'm hoping she'll whip her into shape soon enough."

I smirk. Good luck with that, Chuck. If the limited interactions I've had with her are any indication, Jasmine heels to *no one*. It's one of the main reasons I find her so intriguing.

"If Madeline can't handle it, I'm sure Kingston here would be *more than happy* to show her how things work around here," my dad offers. "Right, son?"

I swallow the remaining liquid in my glass before nodding. "Of course. I would *love* to put her in her place. I met her this morning and I can certainly appreciate your problem, Charles. She's rather... spirited."

He lifts an eyebrow. "Do you really think you could break her of that stupid notion?"

Both men are watching me carefully, waiting for my response.

I give them a confident grin, despite the fact that confidence is the last thing I'm feeling right now. "Without a doubt. In fact, I'd be happy to start right away. By the time I'm done with her, she'll be the most obedient woman you know."

Charles' eyes light up. "I knew you were special,

son." He turns toward my dad. "If he does well with this, maybe we should bring him in on *other* projects."

My father nods. "Agreed. I think it's about time."

Well, well. It looks like I may not need Peyton after all.

chapter seven

JAZZ

At quarter to six, Ms. Williams showed up at my door to ensure I was dressed properly. Apparently, the sperm donor didn't trust me to do it myself, which was actually pretty smart of him if I'm being honest. After donning the green Prada dress and gold sandals she pulled out of my closet, I'm being ushered to the formal dining room.

When I hesitate at the bottom of the staircase, she gives me a little shove. "Hurry, now. The Davenports have been here for a while and they should be finished with pre-dinner drinks. Your father does not tolerate tardiness."

I have a feeling he doesn't tolerate much of anything.

When I arrive, Madeline, Peyton, and the third—or

fourth—Mrs. Davenport are sitting at the table, sipping on champagne.

"Oh, Jasmine, there you are!" Madeline motions me over. "This is Vanessa Davenport, honey. Come say hello."

I nod to the pretty blonde who couldn't possibly be over twenty-five. "Nice to meet you, Mrs. Davenport."

She stands and does this weird air kiss thing on each side of my face. "Oh, my, you're absolutely gorgeous!" Mrs. Davenport faces Madeline. "Maddie, you didn't mention how beautiful she was. Charles must be so proud."

Yeah, because a woman's value is in her beauty, right?

"Thanks," I mumble, reminding myself this woman has done nothing wrong to me.

Right before I sit down, three men enter the room.

"Preston, come here and meet Jasmine." Vanessa practically pushes me toward her husband. What is it with these people and the pushing? "Isn't she lovely? God, what I wouldn't give to have skin this flawless!"

I'm positioned in front of a tall, attractive man who's assessing me carefully. I get the feeling he's expecting me to be some mousy little thing, so I make a point to hold my chin high and look him directly in the eye. Well, when his eyes finally make their way up to my face anyway. The longer I stand here, the more I see how much he resembles his son. This Preston guy is basically Kingston in thirty years.

I resist the urge to flinch when he grabs my hand and brings it to his mouth for a kiss. "Why, yes, Vanessa. She is *quite* a beautiful young woman. It's *very* nice to meet you, Jasmine."

Bile rises in my throat when he starts stroking the underside of my wrist with his index finger.

I pull away quickly and step back. "Thanks."

I glance up and see his son coming from behind him. If I'm not mistaken, Kingston doesn't seem happy with his dad right now.

"Father, if you'll excuse me so I can take my seat."

His dad laughs. "Of course, of course. Please forgive me for causing a traffic jam. You know how irresistible I find a beautiful woman."

Sperm Donor pats the pervert on the back. "It happens to the best of us, Preston."

Everyone in the room chuckles except for me. Correction—Kingston's too busy swallowing the amber liquid one of the maids just set before him.

I take a seat, thankfully in a spot far away from Mr. Davenport. Not so thankfully, the only empty chair with food in front of it was the one occupied by the other Davenport male. I risk a glance at him and his lips turn up in the corners, as if he knows how uncomfortable I am.

Fuck you, my eyes say.

He raises an absurdly sexy eyebrow before leaning into my ear. "Something on your mind, *Jazz*? You seem tense. Would you like me to help you *relax*?"

What the hell? I'd expect that comment from his horny friend, but I didn't think Kingston Davenport was capable of being flirty. This has to be some new form of torment since he's made it clear that's his goal. Game on, dickhead.

I lean into his ear. "I can *relax* just fine all by myself. If I do ever need assistance, I'm sure your friend, Bentley, wouldn't mind filling in." Kingston tenses when I dig my nails into his forearm. "I will admit, that bulge of his has me curious to see if it's as impressive as it seemed in Lit class."

"Stay away from Bentley," he growls.

"Why would I—"

"Baby," Peyton whines, tugging on his other arm. "Did you hear me?"

I sit back in my chair and casually take a sip of water.

Kingston glances at me one more time before turning his attention to my stepsister. "What do you want, Peyton?"

She trails a finger up his arm. "I asked if you wanted to stay for a while after dinner. I miss you, baby."

His jaw tics. "How many times do we have to discuss this? It's *not* happening."

Peyton glances toward me, probably to see if I'm paying attention.

I lift an eyebrow. "Oh, don't mind me. I'm just here for the food."

She glares. "Stay out of it, whore."

I hold my palms up. "I couldn't care less what either one of you do."

Peyton presses her huge boobs into Kingston's side. "C'mon, baby, let me take care of you. It's been *so* long. I'll even let you stick it up *you know where*."

She looks directly at me as she says this, like she thinks I'd be jealous or something. One might think anal sex was a rather bold topic for Peyton to bring up in front of the parents, but we're on the opposite end of a table that seats at least thirty. It's the rich person's version of a kiddie table, I suppose. She's being quiet enough that her voice won't carry, but it's obvious she wants me to hear this for some reason.

Kingston scoffs. "I'd rather have my dick rot off than *ever* put it inside you again."

I don't even try to hide my laughter which makes Peyton fume. I don't think she was expecting such a venomous response, and she certainly didn't want me to witness it.

She discreetly flips me off before turning her attention back to Kingston. "Maybe I'll go see Lucas Gale. He's *always* interested."

Kingston rolls his eyes. "Knock yourself out. Tell him I send my condolences."

Peyton sits back and crosses her arms over her chest. "Ugh, whatever."

Man, what the hell is up with these two? I guess

Ainsley was right—their *relationship* is for appearances only. My question is, why bother?

If I thought dinner my first night here was awkward, it was nothing compared to this. Throughout the rest of the meal, I sit back and stockpile information. I'm a people watcher—always have been. You can learn a lot about someone's true self by simply paying attention. And *these* people are definitely trying to hide something. Thankfully, they're all so self-absorbed, nobody notices I'm not talking, nor do they try to engage me in conversation.

It's so obvious they can't stand each other. As Charles and Mr. Davenport discuss boating, or golfing, or how well their businesses are doing, you can see their minds working, trying to figure out what to say next to best the other. The two wives at the table are all smiles and laughter, but when Mrs. Davenport looks away, Madeline rolls her eyes, glares at Sperm Donor, or sends longing looks in Mr. Davenport's direction. Mrs. Davenport has her own set of wandering eyes when she thinks no one is watching, although hers are directed toward her stepson. Huh. That's... *interesting*.

As for Peyton and Kingston, those two are probably the worst. Every single time Peyton opens her mouth, Kingston's fist clenches on his lap. When she asks him a question, he answers with as few words as possible. If she's complaining about something or belittling someone—which takes up practically the entire conversation—Kingston scoffs or flat-out ignores her. Peyton doesn't seem to notice he hasn't made any effort as she prattles on and on. Or maybe she just doesn't care. I wouldn't be surprised by either.

I can't get back to my room fast enough once the final course is cleared. God, why would anyone want to live like that? They're all so toxic to one another. Are appearances really that important?

～

After taking a shower, I walk out of the bathroom and scream when I see the hulking figure sitting on my bed. His lips tilt in a smug grin, clearly pleased with himself for frightening me. My eyes hone in on muscular arms as he folds them behind his head, relaxing as if he has every right to be on my bed. God, he really is a perfect specimen of the male species. Broad shoulders, ripped body, full lips, and a jaw that would make Henry Cavill jealous. How can someone so ugly on the inside be so beautiful on the outside?

Kingston's hazel eyes are his most prominent feature. Not because they're framed by inky black lashes that women pay good money for, more so because of how much depth they hold. No doubt, this guy is hiding some major demons. After meeting his dad earlier, I'd wager that man is a big part of it. As Kingston's gaze bores into me, taking in the fact I'm wearing nothing but a towel, chills race down my spine. Hatred wars with lust as he looks me over, causing all sorts of confusing emotions.

I refuse to let this jerk intimidate me though, so I straighten my spine and return his frosty expression. "What are you doing here, Kingston? How did you even know which room was mine?"

He eyes me with a look so sinister, I almost lose my bravado. "We need to have a little chat."

I make a conscious effort to loosen my limbs as I walk into my closet and start searching for some pajamas. "Unless you're here to apologize for being an asshole, I have no desire to listen to anything you have to say."

I stiffen when I feel his hard body pressed against mine. Crap, how did he move across the room so silently?

"That's *never* going to happen. We might as well get that out of the way."

I jerk my head over my shoulder. "Well, then you can leave."

Before I can even register what's happening, Kingston has me turned around and pressed against the back wall of my closet. He runs the tip of his finger across my exposed collarbone, swiping at the droplets of water left behind from my shower. I bite back a moan as tingles erupt throughout my body, making my toes curl.

He leans down so we're face to face, holding me

captive with his gaze. I challenge him with my defiance, never once looking away. I can smell alcohol on his breath as the heat from his body crashes into mine. I'm hyperaware that only a flimsy towel covers my body as he cages me in. An inferno builds inside of me as we stare at one another, wordlessly communicating something... although I haven't quite figured out *what* that may be yet.

Kingston grips my chin and leans in farther until he's mere inches away from my mouth. "Listen to me carefully, because I'm only going to say this once. Stay the fuck out of my way. I've worked too long and too hard to have some newly discovered bastard screw this up for me."

"What the hell are you talking about?" I fight a wince when his grip tightens. I'm almost certain I'll have fingertip-shaped bruises left behind. "Why can't you just fucking *leave me alone?*"

Kingston's nostrils flare. "Because you distract me."

"*Distract you?* And that's my fault how?"

His eyes narrow into slits. "Don't act like you don't know what you're doing."

My jaw drops. "I'm not doing *anything*! What kind of fucked up world do you live in where you can just bully someone or throw around accusations like this? Are you here on Peyton's behalf? Does she want me gone? Is that what this is about?"

"This has nothing to do with Peyton. I don't give a shit what she wants."

I roll my eyes. "Wow... don't hold your breath waiting for the Boyfriend of the Year Award."

He scoffs. "I'm not her boyfriend and we're all well aware of that."

"Yeah… I really don't think she'd agree. She seemed pretty territorial at dinner."

Kingston's gaze lowers to my lips for a brief moment. "Final warning, *Jazz*."

I laugh mockingly. "Or what? You don't sc—"

I'm cut off mid-sentence when his lips claim mine aggressively, his tongue demanding entrance. I gasp which gives him the opening he needs to invade my mouth. Something stirs inside of me then—something purely primitive—and before I can second guess myself, I kiss him back, hard and hot, practically branding myself on his lips.

Kingston wraps his arms around me and wedges his powerful thigh between mine. Our bodies are pressed together, all of his hard edges against my delicately soft curves. Our breaths mingle while our tongues tangle. There's so much urgency behind this kiss, as if we're trying to crawl inside each other. It's hungry and ferocious. Drugging and dizzying. I had no idea a simple meeting of two peoples' lips could be so damn potent.

Desire thrums through me as his pillowy lips carve a path down my jawline, his teeth scraping along the nape of my neck. Kingston mutters a curse and picks me up, wrapping my legs around his hips. He's tenting his pants, grinding his erection against me.

Kingston bites the spot where my neck meets my shoulder. "You like that?"

My spine bows. "Yeah."

He groans as his fingers slip beneath the towel, finding my hot flesh. "You want more?"

My head falls back as my eyes close. "Yeah."

If I was capable of rational thought right now, his dark chuckle might bother me, but I *can't* think at the moment—I can only feel. I've been so numb over the last few weeks, I latch on to this high like it's my lifeline. I shudder when he brushes his fingers through my wetness. Groan as he inserts one long finger inside of me. Kingston's breath hitches as he pumps his finger in and out, rubbing the heel of his palm against my clit.

I bite my bottom lip when he adds a second finger. Together, we develop a rhythm that screams of desperation and hunger. He studies my face, carefully cataloging each feature. Kingston is so perfectly in tune with my whimpers and moans—adjusting angles, pressure, and speed to deliver the most pleasure. It's so intense, I come apart in record time. He slows his movements as I writhe against him before withdrawing completely. It's shocking how bereft I suddenly feel as he pulls away, putting my feet back on solid ground.

When our eyes meet, he looks as stunned as I feel. His sandy hair is askew, his breathing is ragged, and his eyes are wild. There's an obvious bulge in his slacks, but that seems to be the least of his concerns. Before I can utter a single word, Kingston marches out of my room, slamming the door behind him. The moment he's gone, I glide down the wall, my legs too jelly-like to remain standing. As I comb my hands through my hair, I replay the last ten minutes in my head.

What in the ever-loving hell was that?

chapter eight

JAZZ

"What is going on with you and my brother?" Ainsley asks during lunch. "He's been throwing shade at Peyton all morning and he won't stop staring at you."

I almost choke on my pasta primavera. "*Nothing* is going on between me and your brother."

Ainsley gives me a skeptical look. "Jazz, seriously. Don't tell me 'nothing' because my twin senses are tingling. Yesterday Kingston was a major dick to you and now he looks like he wants to jump your bones. Also, you have the fact that he's not even trying to hide his contempt toward Peyton. What the hell happened at dinner last night?"

I shrug. "*Nothing* happened."

"That's bullshit. He wants something from you." She pauses for a moment. "Or he already *got* something from you."

I try fighting it, but I know I'm blushing. I can only hope my tanned complexion hides it. I can't stop thinking about what happened in my closet last night. I'm no virgin, but I'm not a girl who easily jumps into bed with someone. I've only slept with one guy, and he was my boyfriend. The fact I allowed Kingston to touch me like that when I just met him is completely out of character for me. Why do I have to be so damn attracted to him? And why did it have to feel so good?

Ainsley gasps. "Oh my God, that's it, isn't it?" She leans over and lowers her voice even more. "Did you two hook up last night?"

"No, we didn't hook up!" I whisper-shout. "Just please drop it, Ainsley."

She looks over my shoulder. "Oh, this ought to be good."

I turn around. "What ought to be—"

My question is answered when I see Peyton and Kingston having a heated discussion. Her face is pinched and her arms are flailing. I turn back around when she jumps out of her chair and marches directly toward me.

Ainsley smiles sweetly when Peyton arrives at our table. "Oh, hey, Peyton. What's up?"

Peyton parks a hand on her hip and glares at me. "Stay out of this, Ainsley. My problem is with *that bitch.*"

Did Kingston tell her about what happened last night?

I fold my arms, trying to appear disinterested. "Watch who you're calling a bitch, *bitch*."

I don't mean to, but I look back at Kingston. He's watching our interaction carefully but making no move to interfere.

She mimics my pose. "Stop staring at my boyfriend. It's pathetic."

"Pathetic?" I scoff. "What's *pathetic* is the fact you're so delusional you can't see *I'm* not the one with a staring problem. You should be having this discussion with your so-called boyfriend."

Her blue eyes flash with ire as her face reddens. "Kingston is *mine*, you whore. Stay away from him."

I smirk. "I have no interest in being anywhere near Kingston. You should be telling *him* to stay away from *me*."

"Yeah, right. Like that's necessary." Peyton cocks her head and twirls her finger in my direction. "Trash isn't his type."

I lift my eyebrows, ignoring her jab. "You sure about that?"

I can see the doubt set in right before a huge grin stretches across her face. "You know what? You're right. Why are we even having this conversation? You're my sister. The last thing we should be doing is fighting over a stupid boy."

I scrub a hand over my face. Is this chick mental? Does she not remember warning me to stay away from her boyfriend within the first few minutes of meeting me?

"Jazz, look o—" Ainsley tries to warn me, but it's too late.

I lift my head just in time to feel ice cold water raining down on me. Laughter echoes throughout the room, growing so loud it's almost deafening. Peyton is grinning with my now empty glass in her hand. Okay, that's it; I've officially had enough.

I bolt out of my chair and punch Peyton right in the face. My lips curl at the satisfying crunch my fist makes. Screams break out as blood sprays from Peyton's nose, little spatters landing on both of our stark white shirts.

"I just got this nose, you skank!" She launches herself at me but my reflexes are on point so I dodge her move.

The floor is slippery from the spilled drink and we both fall down. Peyton and I grapple until I manage to climb over her and straddle her chest. I couldn't care less that my skirt is riding up as I do. Chants of "Girl fight!" ring out amongst our gathered audience, but I do my best to focus on the target at hand. I deliver a swift bitch slap right across Peyton's cheek before clenching her shirt in my hand.

Her eyes widen in panic as I put pressure on her chest, getting right in her face. "I fucking warned you, bitch, but you didn't listen. I was happy to leave you alone but if you want to fuck with me, I'm *going* to fight back and I'm going to fight *dirty*."

A set of strong arms loop under my armpits, hauling me off of her.

"That's enough!" a deep voice growls.

I shrug out of Kingston's hold and pin him with a glare. "Don't fucking touch me!"

"You'll pay for this!" Peyton screams as she stands. "You're fucking dead, you stupid cunt!"

I lunge for her again, but I'm held back by a different set of arms. "Whoa there, kitten. Retract the claws."

I look over my shoulder and find Bentley, his brown eyes twinkling in amusement. "Let. Me. Go."

He tightens his grip. "Nah, I'm good."

I jab my heel into his shin repeatedly, eliciting a few "Oofs!" but the bastard doesn't relinquish his hold.

Peyton is trying to get to me as well while Kingston restrains her. She's tossing out all kinds of threats but I tune her out.

"Enough!" a loud, authoritative voice booms. "Somebody escort Miss Devereux to the infirmary." The fifty-something balding man walks up to me, scowling in disapproval. "As for you, Miss Callahan, get cleaned up and report directly to my office."

I throw my hands up as Bentley releases me. "What? She started it! And who the hell are you anyway?"

A round of snickers passes through the crowd.

The man narrows his beady eyes. "I'm *Headmaster* Davis. And *you* are not getting off to a good start, young lady. You have exactly twenty minutes to get cleaned up."

The man storms out of the dining room without another word.

"Shit, new girl," Bentley says as he swings his heavy arm over my shoulder. "That was hot AF, but you're in deep shit. The headmaster don't play when people throw punches on campus. You gotta save that shit for when there're no witnesses." He leans into my ear. "Nice panties, by the way. Lace looks good on you."

I push his arm off. "Pig."

He winks. "Oink, oink, baby."

Ainsley weaves in between us. "Move, Bentley. Are you okay, Jazz?"

I pull my long hair over my shoulder and wring it out over the floor. "I'm fine. Stupid bitch wouldn't know how to throw a solid punch if her life depended on it."

Ainsley's eyes widen as she shucks off her blazer. "I have a spare uniform in my locker that you can borrow. Here, put this on for now."

I follow her gaze and sure enough, my white dress shirt is completely see-through. And of course, I'm wearing a sheer red bra because my shirt is thick enough that it wasn't a problem when it was dry. Now, not so much. As I'm buttoning Ainsley's jacket, I make the mistake of looking up to find three sets of eyes staring at my chest.

I narrow my eyes at Kingston, Reed, and Bentley. "Grow up, dickheads. They're nipples—we all have them."

Kingston returns my glare, Bentley wags his eyebrows and winks, and Reed looks like he couldn't possibly be more bored, which seems to be his default setting.

I roll my eyes when I see Whitney and Imogen fawning all over my stepsister as the three of them exit the room. I have no doubt Peyton's going to play the victim card and milk this for all it's worth.

Now that the fight is over, the other students return to their tables and resume eating their lunch as if nothing happened.

I turn to leave, but Kingston steps in front of me, blocking my path. "Dumb move, Jasmine."

I flip him off. "Fuck you and fuck your bitch ass girlfriend. You two deserve each other."

I grab Ainsley's elbow. "Let's get the hell out of here."

chapter nine

JAZZ

"I am sorely disappointed in you, young lady. It's bad enough you injured your sister, but you embarrassed this family." Sperm Donor frowns. "How am I supposed to explain why any daughter of mine would behave like this?"

Charles summoned me to his study the moment he got home. He's been reading me the riot act for the past five minutes, and it's taking everything in me to remain calm.

"Oh, I don't know. Maybe the fact that Peyton started it by dumping ice water all over me."

Charles leans back in his chair. "She said it was an accident."

I scoff. "Really? She *accidentally* picked up my water glass, *accidentally* raised it above my head, and *accidentally* flipped it over? You can't possibly believe that."

"Why would she lie? Peyton has zero history of violence." He opens the top drawer of his desk and pulls out a file. "According to this, you cannot say the same."

I crane my neck, trying to see what's in the folder. "What is that?"

He flips through some papers. "A standard dossier. School records, housing records, criminal background check. This isn't the first time you've been in a physical altercation at school."

What the fuck? Who the hell keeps a file on their kid?

"I was in *one* fight at school and I didn't start that one either."

Some chick at my old school didn't like the way her boyfriend looked at me, so she decided to throw down in the middle of PE.

He levels me with an icy stare. "You're lucky Headmaster Davis was so understanding about your upbringing and agreed to limit your punishment to detention. Windsor Academy typically has a zero-tolerance policy on violence. I had to make a generous donation to convince him to look the other way. You will *not* get another chance, so I suggest you figure out a way to stay out of trouble. If you get expelled from Windsor, I'll have to ship you off to a boarding school."

My jaw drops. "Why can't I just go to public school? It's not like the school system here sucks."

"No child of mine will go to *public school*." He says

the last two words with a sour look on his face. "You'll either attend Windsor or I'm shipping you off. I have contacts at an academy in Connecticut. I'm sure we can get you in there."

I shake my head. "I can't leave LA. I *won't* leave my sister. My *real* sister."

Charles gives me a contemptuous smile. "Well, then I guess you'll need to behave yourself, won't you? Do we have an understanding, Jasmine?"

I roll my tongue in my cheek. "Yeah, I understand."

I understand you're an even bigger asshole than I originally thought.

He nods. "Good. Now, get the hell out of my office so I can get back to work."

Gladly, you prick.

~

I desperately need to hear Belle's voice, so I pick up my phone and pull up her father's contact info.

He answers on the third ring. "Yeah?"

"Hey, Jerome. This is Jazz."

"What do you want?" he slurs.

Great. He's been drinking.

I take a seat on the edge of my bed. "I was hoping I could speak with Belle."

"Can't. Monica is giving her a bath and shit."

"Who's Monica?"

"My woman. What's it to you?"

Well, at least Belle isn't alone with this loser. Hopefully Monica is much nicer than he is. And more sober.

"Um... I just really miss her and wanted to check in. I called the other day, but I hadn't heard back yet."

"I've been busy."

Busy finding the bottom of a bottle, I'm sure.

"You still working construction, Jerome?"

"Nah," he says. "Boss man didn't like it when I cut out early one day and told me to not bother coming back."

"So, what are you doing for work now?"

"What's it to you?"

"I want to make sure my sister is being taken care of."

It sounds like he's taking a drag from a cigarette. "Don't you worry your pretty little head about us, sweetheart. Monica's a good woman. Can't have kids of her own so she's been takin' care of Belle real good."

"I'd like to see her this weekend. I can come to you if that makes it easier."

"Sure, sure. Just give me a call and we'll set something up."

I crinkle my brows. "Um... can we just set something up now since I have you on the phone?"

"No can do. Real busy here. We'll talk later."

"Wait!" I want to scream when the call disconnects.

I consider calling back, but I know Jerome would just ignore it. I never understood how he and my mom got together in the first place. Sure, he's a quintessential tall, dark, and handsome man, but he's a drunk and a jerk. Mom swore he was sober when they met and quite charming. Supposedly, he didn't start drinking heavily until she was pregnant. Personally, I think he was just better at hiding it before then.

Now that I think about it, I wonder what the hell she saw in my sperm donor. So far, I haven't seen any redeeming qualities. Mom once told me she worked for him, but she wouldn't divulge anything else, afraid to give me any information that would reveal his identity. I was shocked when I learned his name was added to my birth certificate.

My social worker, Davina, made a solid point—if my mom truly didn't want me to find him, why would she do that? Things just aren't adding up. I need to sit down with Charles and get his side of the story. It's probably best if I give him some time to cool off. Maybe by the time Peyton's nose is better, he'll be more willing to talk to me about it. I have to at least try. It's not like I can get answers from the grave.

chapter ten

JAZZ

The rest of the week is a complete clusterfuck. It seems as if the entire school has turned on me besides Ainsley. I've been called every derogatory name under the sun by people I've never met, had countless others try to trip me, shoulder check me, or shoot spitballs into my hair. The only time someone doesn't pick on me, is during lunch. The fact that Headmaster Davis is constantly making rounds through the dining room since the fight probably has something to do with that.

By the time Friday rolls around, I can't wait for the final bell so I can have a break from this hellhole. I'm actually looking forward to what the weekend has in store. I consider checking out the pool since I practically have that giant house to myself. Charles went away on business again and Madeline and Peyton have gone to a spa in San Francisco, or whatever that's code for. At home, it's just me and the staff who are pretty much invisible unless you need something from them. Jerome still won't return my calls, but I'm going to keep trying until he does. Worst case scenario, I'll call our social worker and see if I can convince her to give me Belle's address.

Considering how cold people have been to me, I'm stunned when Bentley comes up to my locker right before first period and swings his arm around me. "Jazzy Jazz, how are you doing this fine morning?"

I try pulling away, but he grips my shoulder, holding me in place. "Get off me."

He leans down and whispers, "Aw, c'mon baby, don't be like that. You let Kingston get up in that pretty pussy. Don't you think I should have a taste?"

Wait... what?

I rear back and I'm sure my confusion is evident. "What are you talking about?"

He presses his free hand over his heart. "Oh, you thought he'd keep that to himself? Like maybe it meant something to him? That's adorable."

I scoff. "Fuck off."

Bentley laughs. "Remember what I said about you talking dirty? It makes me hard."

I give him the stink-eye. "Anything with tits makes you hard."

He mock shivers. "Not true. I can think of quite a few women in my life who have the opposite effect. Take Ms. Henderson, for example. Major boner killer."

I snort. Ms. Henderson has blueish gray hair, leather skin, and is approximately one-hundred-and-eighty years old. I continue walking down the hall, his heavy arm weighing me down. I don't miss the dirty looks pretty much every girl in the vicinity is giving me. I stop when we get to my first class.

"Bentley, I need to get to class."

Right when I think he's going to let me go, he pulls me into him instead. My nose is smashed against his chest as he envelops me in a bear hug. I'm not proud to admit it, but I make no attempt to retreat. Everyone can use a hug sometimes, and I'm definitely overdue.

He kisses me on the cheek. "See you later, babe."

I place my hand over the spot his lips just touched as I watch him walk away. I must've been in a daze because I don't notice anyone approaching me until I'm clipped in the shoulder.

"Move out of the way, bitch," Whitney sneers as she walks past me to take her seat.

Great. Now another one of the Queen Bs has a problem with me. I take my seat and look straight ahead, waiting for class to begin. I can feel people staring, but I ignore them. Hell, I'm actually getting used to it by now, as sad as that is.

My head turns when someone kicks my chair.

The girl who sits behind me—Jessica, I think—smiles. "Oops, my bad."

I roll my eyes as I turn back around. The entire class is filled with one taunt after another by Whitney and several of our classmates. Our teacher is oblivious, and I can't help but wonder if that's intentional or not. These bitches aren't exactly being quiet with their name-calling. Slut, trash, cum bucket—their insults are disguised by fake sneezes or coughs, but the words couldn't be any clearer.

I stay seated after the bell rings, waiting for the other students to file out, so I don't have to be in the middle of them.

Whitney pauses next to my desk and grins. "If you don't stay away from the kings—especially Bentley—this is just the beginning, whore." She knocks my backpack off my chair and saunters out the door with a little extra pep.

I grit my teeth, fuming, as she leaves the classroom. I remind myself that I cannot go after her or I'll be facing expulsion. And if I get expelled, Charles will ship me off to Connecticut, where I have no chance of seeing my sister.

~

Ainsley practically pounces on me the moment I sit down for lunch. "There's a party tonight and you're coming with me."

I laugh. "Uh... no, I'm not. I have no desire to spend extra time with these assholes."

She pouts. "C'mon, Jazz, it'll be fun! Donovan, the guy who's throwing it, is funny and sexy and sweet.

And best of all, he's in college so I highly doubt many high schoolers will be there."

Ainsley gets a dreamy look in her eyes when she mentions this Donovan guy.

"You like him, don't you?"

She smiles. "I really do. He's a freshman at UCLA but he went to Windsor which is how I met him. I had the biggest crush on him last year but he had a girlfriend. I ran into him at the Commons yesterday and he invited me. And get this—he just happened to mention that he's single now! That's gotta be a hint, right?"

"It does sound like he's into you," I agreed. "What's the Commons?"

"Oh, it's kind of like the central meeting spot nearby. I totally had a craving for sushi after ballet, so I stopped there for dinner last night. They have *the best* sushi place. Donovan was there too—looking even hotter than he was last year—and we wound up sitting together and talking for like two hours." She puts her hands in a prayer position. "Please, please, please come with me, Jazz. I don't want to show up alone just in case I was reading him wrong. If we get there and you absolutely hate it, I promise we'll leave right away."

I sigh. "Fine."

She beams. "I'll pick you up at six. We can grab a bite to eat and get ready at my house. You can even sleep over if you want. Don't worry about my jerkface brother; he lives in the pool house and he's usually at Reed's or Bentley's on the weekends."

"What exactly do I need to get *ready* for?"

Ainsley gives me an *Are you dense?* look. "Because there's going to be a bunch of hot college guys there! Consider this your chance to let loose and act your age. Have a few drinks, maybe flirt with a few guys. Just set aside all the crappy stuff for one night and have fun. I really think you need this, Jazz. You can't be sad or angry all the time. It's not healthy."

"Am I that obvious?"

She gives me a sad smile in reply.

I take a deep breath. "Okay, you're right. What harm can letting loose for one night cause? I'm in."

chapter eleven

JAZZ

Famous last words.

That's the first thing I think when I walk into the party. Pure pandemonium, that's what this is. Donovan's place is packed with bodies, all in various states of intoxication. I've been to plenty of ragers over the last few years, but this is on a whole other level. I've never seen so much excess in one place.

There's an elaborate bar set up in one corner and a DJ booth in another, pumping beats through a kickass sound system. Scantily clad girls are grinding on a makeshift dance floor, surrounded by a group of guys watching them appreciatively. Couples are making out against every available surface—a few even appear to be doing *a lot* more than kissing, with no regards to their audience. A cloud of smoke circles a group of people taking hits from a bong while others sitting with them are snorting lines of white powder using rolled up bills.

I shake my head when the song switches and Kendrick Lamar begins rapping about being humble. That would be the last word I'd use to describe any of these people.

"This is great, right?" Ainsley yells into my ear, looking around excitedly.

"Yeah... sure."

She points to the bar area. "Let's get a drink."

We walk up to the bar where there's an actual bartender manning the station.

His green eyes sparkle with interest as he checks me out. "What can I get you pretty ladies?"

Ainsley smiles. "Give me a screwdriver."

Bartender guy turns to me. "And you, beautiful?"

"I'll have a screwdriver as well."

"Coming right up." He grabs two red Solo cups and pours a generous amount of vodka into each before adding some OJ. His fingertips graze mine as he hands me a drink, and I blush. "I'm Kyle. You just let me know if you need anything else." Kyle looks to be in his early twenties, so I'm guessing this might be a part-time job for him while he's in college.

I bite my lip before taking a sip. "Thanks, Kyle. I'm Jazz."

He raises an eyebrow. "You come here for someone in particular? Or *with* someone?"

Ainsley smiles knowingly. "You askin' if my girl here is available?"

Kyle laughs. "Maybe I am." His eyes never leave mine as he answers her question. "So... are you available, Jazz?"

"Oh, um... I guess you—"

"I'm fairly certain you're being paid to mix drinks, not pick up women," an all too familiar deep voice growls from my right.

Kingston has wedged himself between me and Ainsley, looking far too good for my comfort. His navy t-shirt is molded to the muscles that lay beneath and his dark fitted jeans hang low off his hips. He's wearing a pair of white Jordans that don't have a scuff on them. I wouldn't be surprised if he just pulled them out of the box.

Kyle straightens his spine and clears his throat. "What can I get you, man?"

"Macallan." Kingston levels Kyle with a glare. "And make it fucking snappy."

"Stop being a dick!" Ainsley smacks her brother's arm. "What the hell are you doing here anyway?"

Kingston ignores her and scowls at the bartender while he's fixing his drink. When Kyle passes the scotch over to him, Kingston doesn't even acknowledge him. Just downs the shot and slams the cup back down.

Kingston grabs both me and Ainsley by the elbow, leading us away.

"Hey!" I shout.

"What the hell?" Ainsley gripes at the same time.

He releases us once we're a good twenty feet away. "The better question is, what the hell are you two doing here?"

Ainsley crosses her arms over her chest. "We were invited."

Kingston's lips curl as his attention turns to me. "Well, look at that; the trash is playing dress up."

Insult aside, he's right in one respect—I definitely don't look like myself right now. By the time Ainsley was finished with me, my eye makeup was all smoky sex kitten, my long hair was pin-straight, and my clothes were... well, they're kind of toeing the line between skanky and sexy. But if I'm being honest, I like the idea of getting out of my own skin for a night. I thought maybe if I didn't look like myself, I could temporarily forget about all the depressing shit in my life.

My eyes narrow into slits. "Fuck you."

His face lights up in a mocking grin. "Not if yours was the last pussy on Earth, sweetheart."

Really? my eyes say. *It didn't seem that way the other night.*

I didn't hear you complaining, his eyes retort.

I have to remind myself not to shrivel under his scrutiny as his gaze leisurely runs the length of my body. I have no doubt he's doing it to make me uncomfortable, and I refuse to give him that satisfaction.

When he pauses on my chest, I look down to make sure nothing is popping out. My boobs aren't big—slightly less than a handful—but the tight black tank Ainsley convinced me to wear has a low neckline and cut outs which expose a little side boob.

The muscles in his neck tighten. "Was your little pet project also invited?"

Ainsley rolls her eyes. "Lay off, Kingston."

"I'll *lay off* when you stop being a stubborn—"

We're interrupted when some guy joins us, obviously checking Ainsley out. "You made it!"

Every trace of irritation from fighting with her brother vanishes. "Donovan!" She nods to me. "This is my friend, Jazz. I hope it's okay I brought her along."

He flashes a toothy smile. "Of course it's okay. Beautiful women are always welcome in my house." Donovan nods to Kingston. "You come with your sister, too?"

Kingston shakes his head. "Nah, Reed and Bent are around here somewhere."

Donovan swings his heavy arms over both mine and Ainsley's shoulders. "Well, then you won't mind if I steal these beauties, will ya?"

Kingston's jaw tics. "Knock yourself out, man."

Donovan leads us toward the wall of sliding glass doors. "Let's head out back. It's much more chill out there."

"Sounds good to me." Ainsley giggles.

I slip out of his hold—which he doesn't even seem

to notice—and follow them outside. We make our way to a large firepit surrounded by long, wooden benches. Donovan pulls Ainsley onto his lap, burying his nose in her neck. I smile when I see how positively gleeful my friend is right now. This guy is definitely into her, and he's making a pretty public statement about it.

A different guy takes a seat on my left. "You're new around here. I would've remembered seeing someone as beautiful as you."

I take a sip of my drink before replying. This guy's good looking, in a preppy kind of way. Tall, brown hair, green eyes, nice smile.

"I am. You a friend of Donovan's?"

"I am." His smile widens, which makes two dimples pop, adding to his all-American boy appeal. "I'm Lawson. And you are...?"

I grin. "Jazz."

Lawson takes my hand and places a kiss on top. "It's very nice to meet you, Jazz. So, where are you from?"

"LA. Watts area, to be more specific."

Lawson lifts his eyebrows in surprise. "Quite the upgrade."

"Depends who you ask, I suppose." I shrug. Thinking about home makes me think about my mom, so I quickly change the subject. "Do you go to UCLA?"

He nods. "I do—freshman year. What about you?"

"Uh... I'm at Windsor Academy right now. Senior year."

"I know Windsor well. Graduated last year." He scoots a little closer. "How do you like it so far?"

"The school seems all right. Most of the student body, not so much."

Lawson laughs. "That good, huh? I can't imagine a pretty girl like you has any trouble fitting in."

"Well, then you'd be surprised."

Lawson and I make small talk for a while before he jerks his head to the right. "You interested in taking a dip in the hot tub?"

On the other end of the deck, there's a huge hot tub sitting under a pergola lined with mini Edison bulbs. There's only one couple in it, but they're going at it pretty hot and heavy.

I point to them. "I don't know if they'd enjoy the company."

He follows my gaze and laughs. "I'm pretty sure they won't even notice we're there."

I raise my brows when the girl pulls back and I catch a glimpse of their faces. She's grinding on top of the guy beneath her—God only knows if either one of them are wearing anything under the waterline. Couples having sex at a party wouldn't normally faze me, but in this case, when the guy is Kingston Davenport and the girl is most definitely *not* Peyton, it gets my attention. I'm not deluding myself into thinking what happened in my closet the other day meant anything to him, but damn, how many girls does he hook up with?

Right before I'm about to look away, our gazes meet. I can see the muscles in his arms flexing, the same way they did when he had his hand under my towel. The brunette writhing on his lap is moaning loudly now, leaving no question as to what his hand is doing under the water. My face flushes in rage, and maybe a little bit of arousal, as my body remembers exactly how talented his fingers are.

Kingston's lips form into a wicked grin as my eyes narrow on him. I could swear he's challenging me right now—that for some reason he's doing this to make a point. Why the hell would I care who he hooks up with? He's not my boyfriend nor do I *ever* want him to be my boyfriend. So, why do I feel like walking over there and dragging her off of him by her hair?

I take the final sip of my drink and set the cup on the bench. Turning to Lawson, I say, "You know what? I think I'd like to get another drink instead. Do you want to head up to the bar with me?"

Lawson stands up and offers his hand. "That's a great idea, beautiful."

I go to tell Ainsley where I'm going, but she's too busy making out with Donovan.

Lawson leads me back inside, still holding onto my hand. Kyle, the bartender's face falls when he sees us approaching him together.

"Jazz, back so soon. Another screwdriver?"

I smile. "Yes, please."

Kyle nods to Lawson. "And you, buddy?"

"Another beer would be great."

I can't seem to get the image of Kingston and his mystery girl out of my mind. I think I need a quick breather to gather my wits.

I tap Lawson's shoulder. "Hey, would you mind grabbing my drink when it's ready? I'm going to find a bathroom."

"No problem." He points down the long hallway off to the right. "The closest bathroom is down that hall, second door on your left."

I nod. "Thanks. I'll be right back."

There're a few people waiting in line, so I stand with my back pressed against the wall, taking deep breaths. Once my turn is finally up, I lock the door behind me and run my wrists under cold water.

I look at my reflection in the mirror. "Don't let that asshole get to you, Jazz. He's trying to get a reaction out of you. Don't let him win."

Pep talk over, I quickly pee and wash my hands before exiting the room. Lawson is waiting for me right outside the door, two drinks in hand.

"Your drink, milady." He winks as he hands the cup over.

"Thanks." I take a small sip. "You wanna head back outside?"

He crooks his elbow, offering it to me. "I'd be happy to."

When we step through the doors, I make a conscious effort not to turn my head in the direction of the hot tub. Lawson and I head back over to the firepit, but Ainsley and Donovan are nowhere to be found.

"They're upstairs in Donovan's room," Lawson offers. "Your friend asked me to tell you on her behalf."

I bite my lip, slightly irritated that Ainsley would just leave like that without talking to me directly. Then I remember, I did the same to her because I didn't want to interrupt her make-out session. She had no way of knowing I planned on only being gone for a few minutes.

"Right." I release a sigh.

We both take a seat and nurse our drinks while we chat.

After I finish my second drink, he nudges me. "Hey, you want to dance?"

"Sure."

When I start walking toward the house, Lawson grabs my hand to steady me. Damn, I'm really feeling the alcohol. Normally it takes at least three or four before I feel this buzzed. Kyle must've made the second round a bit stronger.

"I was hoping we could have our own little dance party." When I hesitate, he adds, "Just over by the pool house. We'll still be able to hear the music; it just won't be as loud."

I look around and see partygoers spread out. I know better than to be alone with some guy I just met, but we definitely wouldn't be alone if we headed over there.

"Sure."

Lawson leads me to a little patch of garden off to the side of the pool house. The song switches to a slow, sensuous beat right as he pulls me into his arms.

His mouth presses against my ear. "Hi."

I shiver as his hot breath causes goosebumps to scatter across my skin. "Hi."

One song bleeds into a few as Lawson and I dance together. When he spins me around, pressing his front to my back, I can feel his erection digging into my spine. His big hands bracket my hips, which actually helps because my legs are starting to feel like Jell-O.

I whimper when his tongue snakes out and trails down the nape of my neck. "Why don't we take this some place more private?"

I don't think I said yes but Lawson starts leading me to the pool house anyway. When I stumble, he steadies me with a firm hand at my elbow.

"Hold on, baby, we're almost there."

"Lawson, I'm not feeling so hot. I don't think we should—"

He turns the door handle. "It's cool, Jazz. You can just lay down in here until it passes."

I shake my head. "I don't know. I—"

Before I can finish my sentence, another guy comes up beside him.

"Thanks, man." Bentley gives Lawson a fist bump. "I can take it from here."

Lawson winks at me. "She's all yours, Fitzgerald."

What the hell is going on?

"Bentley, what's happening?"

My head suddenly feels too heavy, so I flop it to the side.

He crouches down and brushes some hair away from my face. "Come on, pretty girl, let's get you inside. You're wasted."

I shake my head. "Am not."

He chuckles. "How many drinks have you had?"

I try holding up two fingers, but it takes me a moment to get it. "Just two, but I'm not a lightweight. I think Kyle made my second drink too strong."

His eyebrows pinch together. "Who the fuck is Kyle?"

"The bartender." Why am I slurring?

Bentley picks me up bridal style. "Come on, princess. Let's have a little fun."

I wrap my arms around him and bury my nose into his neck. "Mmm, you smell good." My tongue darts out, tasting his skin. It's salty from a light sheen of sweat, but not unpleasant. "Tastes good, too."

He groans as he shoulders the door open and sets me down. He doesn't let me go though, which is a good thing considering I'm having trouble standing. It's then that I see we're not alone. Kingston and Reed are both standing in the living area.

I glare at Kingston. "Why are *you* here?"

He's dressed now, but his hair is damp and he looks way too good if you ask me.

Kingston gives me a wicked grin. "I'm here to party. Why else would I be here? This is a party, isn't it?"

I turn back to Bentley. "What's this idiot talking about?"

Bentley starts massaging my shoulders, forcing a groan out of me. "Like he said, we're having a party. Our own little *private* party."

My jaw drops as I comprehend the meaning behind his statement. "You're all fucking crazy if you think that's gonna happen."

Bentley brushes my hair aside as his thumbs knead between my shoulder blades. "C'mon, Jazzy, don't be shy now. Kingston told us how hot you were for him. How drenched. How tightly your pretty pink pussy gripped his fingers." His erection digs into my back as he presses into me from behind. "We wanna see how well that pussy can grip our dicks." Bentley's tongue traces a path down the nape of my neck. "How pretty you'd look with all three holes filled."

Oh, God. The image he just planted in my brain is so hot, my entire body flushes. But there's no way in hell I could actually go through with that. Right?

Right?

"I don't..." I shake my head, trying to clear the fog. "I think..."

Bentley moves to my front as someone else takes his place in the back. I know it's Kingston the moment his strong hands grip my hips before making their way up my abdomen.

Bentley frames my face in his hands. "Don't think, Jazzy. Just focus on how good we're gonna make you feel."

Bentley seals his lips over mine right as Kingston's hands cover my breasts. I gasp when Kingston pinches my nipples through the thin fabric of my top, which Bentley takes advantage of by slipping his tongue into my mouth. With the cutouts, my shirt wouldn't allow for a bra, so it's the only thing standing between Kingston's fingers and my skin.

Bentley feasts on my mouth like a man starved, and I give as good as I get. My hands glide under his t-shirt, tracing the muscular planes of his chest. The erection pressed into my stomach jerks when my fingernails rake over his nipple. Behind me, Kingston's hands are everywhere, ratcheting my desire to an almost unbearable level. He lifts my arms straight above my head. My kiss with Bentley is broken as my tank top is pulled over my head and tossed aside.

Bentley groans as he looks at my naked torso. "Fuck, Jazz."

Kingston's large hands cover my breasts and squeeze, rolling my nipples between his index and middle fingers.

My head falls back into his chest. "Oh, God."

"Switch," Kingston demands before coming around to my front while Bentley positions himself in back. Kingston's lids are hooded with lust as he circles my nipple with his finger. My breath hitches as he runs his thumb along my lower lip. He stares at my mouth as my tongue darts out, swirling around the tip. "Fuck."

Kingston grabs my face and without thinking twice, our lips collide. Bentley's tongue is trailing down my neck while my tongue is tangling with Kingston's. Kingston swallows my moan when Bentley bites down, sucking my skin in his retreat. I'm naked from the waist up but they're both still fully clothed. There's something strangely erotic about that but I want more. I'm burning with the need to feel their skin against mine.

I tug on the hem of Kingston's t-shirt. "Take this off." I twist until I'm facing Bentley. "You too. Lose the shirt."

Bentley winks. "You don't need to tell me twice."

Two more shirts join the floor before I'm grabbing the back of Kingston's neck, pulling him into a kiss. As we rub against each other, skin to skin, we're a tornado of sloppy kisses, moans, and deep intakes of breath. Out of the corner of my eye, I see Reed holding his phone up in our direction, but I'm too consumed with lust to question it.

"God, you're so fucking hot." Bentley massages my breasts while licking the shell of my ear.

Kingston breaks away from my mouth and pushes Bentley's hand away before kissing a path down to my left breast. I shudder as his tongue swirls around the pointed tip before sucking it into his mouth. My knees buckle as a wave of dizziness washes over me.

Kingston catches me by the hips as he pulls away. "You okay?"

I shake my head, trying to clear the fog of lust. "Yeah... uh..." Now the room is spinning. "Maybe I should sit down for a minute."

Kingston and Bentley exchange a loaded glance over my shoulder before guiding me to the nearby couch. Man, why am I so sleepy all of a sudden? As my back hits the soft cushions, I curl onto my side.

My lids drift closed. "Just give me a minute and I'll—"

That's the last thing I remember before blacking out.

chapter twelve

KINGSTON

"She's out," Bentley says. "Fuck. That got way out of control. I never would've guessed she'd be that responsive."

I rake my hands through my hair. "Me neither."

I pace the room, needing to distance myself from Jasmine. When we came up with this little plan of ours, Lawson was supposed to deliver her as she was on the verge of passing out. We thought she'd fall asleep, we'd get the pictures we needed, and leave. It seemed that way when she first walked through the door, but she got a second wind when Bent started kissing her. I never intended to take it that far, but once I saw how into it she was, logic took a flying fucking leap out the window.

My fists clench at the thought of Bentley's hands and lips all over her. I don't know what the fuck my problem is—we've shared a few women in the past—but with Jasmine, it's different. *She's* different. There's an obvious spark between the two of them which turned into an inferno tonight. It makes the beast inside of me want to destroy everything in its path.

"I was about to step in and remind you what we were really here for," Reed grumbles. "You fucking idiots let your dicks take charge of that."

I flip him off. "Fuck off, man. I would've stopped it before it got any further."

"Right." He scoffs and holds up his phone. "When you see the video, you may change your mind."

Bentley adjusts himself with a wince. "My boner won't go down. Do I have time for a quick jerk-off sesh?"

I give him a wry look as I move my own dick into a more comfortable position. "Deal with it, asshole. We need to get out of here."

Bentley quickly glances as Jasmine. "What do we do now?"

I motion to the sleeping beauty on the couch. "Let's move to the bedroom. Strip her jeans off and then grab a few pictures to go with the video. We need to hurry in case my sister comes looking for her."

Jasmine stirs slightly as I remove her pants, but she remains asleep. My dick jerks when I catch sight of her red lacy panties and the obvious wet spot on them. Shit. *Focus on the task at hand, asshole.*

Reed snaps some strategically posed pictures of me

and Bentley in bed with Jasmine before we cover her with the blanket. Before we leave, I pull Jasmine's phone out. She has an older model that doesn't have facial recognition. Lucky for me, I spied her passcode when she unlocked it the other day in class. I shoot off a quick text to Ainsley so she knows where to find Jasmine before setting it on the nightstand.

"Let's go."

I let Reed and Bentley go ahead of me before I lock the door and exit the pool house myself. At least a dozen people all watch as we leave with knowing smiles on their faces. They assume we were in there fucking her, and when these pictures get leaked, it will be confirmed. Jasmine Callahan is going to loathe the day she ever set foot on Windsor property.

chapter thirteen

JAZZ

"Jazz, wake up."

I groan as someone shakes me.

"Jazz, c'mon."

I peel my eyes open and squint at the offending sunlight seeping in through the window. Where the hell am I?

"Jazz!"

I turn my head and find Ainsley standing beside the bed I'm in. "Where am I?"

Her brows pinch together. "Donovan's pool house. You don't remember?"

I rub my temples, willing my headache to go away. Ugh, I feel like shit. "I don't remember much of anything." My bare skin rubs against the sheets, startling me. I look under the covers and sure enough, I'm only wearing panties. "Why am I practically naked?"

Ainsley's still frowning. "You seriously don't remember anything? How much did you drink?"

I gingerly sit up, clutching the comforter to my chest. "Only two, but that second one must've been really strong. I remember talking to some guy after you went off with Donovan and not much else."

She picks my phone off the nightstand. "You texted me around one in the morning that you were locking yourself in the pool house to sleep off the liquor."

I grab my phone from her outstretched hand and pull up my messages. Yep, I definitely did that. "Huh. I don't remember any of that."

Her eyes widen. "Did you hook up with someone?"

"What? No!" I would feel it if I had sex, right? I shake my head, internally assessing my body. Nope, I'm definitely not sore down there and my panties are still on, so that's a good sign. Heat floods my core when I remember kissing someone... but that was probably a dream. Hopefully.

Ainsley sighs. "Well, thank God you had the sense to lock the door before you passed out. You can never be too careful."

I smooth down my unruly hair. "How did you get in here?"

She dangles a key chain from her hand. "Donovan gave it to me."

I look around the room and spot my clothes hanging off the chair in the corner. "Would you mind giving me a minute to get dressed?"

Ainsley nods. "Take your time. I'll be up front waiting."

While I'm getting dressed, I glance around the room, trying to jog my memory somehow, but nothing comes. I've never been blackout drunk before, especially after only two drinks. Did that guy I was talking to spike my drink? Ainsley was right; thank God I had the sense to lock myself in here. Who knows what could've happened?

I check the time on my phone as I meet up with Ainsley and see that it's quarter after seven. Shit, how am I going to explain being out all night? Sperm Donor is out of town, but surely Ms. Williams would've tried reaching me. They never set any kind of curfew—or rules in general that don't have to do with appearances —but still. My mom trusted my judgment; if I wanted to stay out late, I did, but she always demanded to know where I was and who I was with. She said it helped ease her mind, knowing she can get to me at any time. Does Charles really not care what happens to me? I guess I'll find out when I get home.

∼

When I walk through the front door after Ainsley dropped me off, there's no one in sight.

"Hello? Is anyone here?"

I startle when Ms. Williams appears out of seemingly nowhere. She eyes me with her usual disgust as she takes in my wrinkled clothes and last night's makeup. "Miss Jasmine. Good morning."

"Good morning," I repeat hesitantly. "Is Charles back in town yet?"

She shakes her head. "No. He's expected to return tomorrow evening."

"Isn't he an attorney? Why is he always out of town? That seems odd to me."

"It's not my job to question Mr. Callahan's where-abouts." Ms. Williams narrows her eyes. "Nor is it yours. Considering you spent the entire night doing God knows what with God knows who, I hardly think you're one to place judgment."

"Wow," I scoff. "I *wasn't* placing judgment; I was just curious. But *you* definitely were."

Ms. Williams huffs. "If you didn't come home looking like you've been working the streets all night, maybe I wouldn't have. Your father will not be pleased when he hears how you're conducting yourself in such a sleazy manner."

"Well, then he can take it up with me when he gets back." I roll my eyes as I march up the stairs.

When I get to my room, I dial Jerome's number again, but he still won't answer. I'd really like to see my sister sometime this weekend, but he's making that rather difficult. *Why* he's making it so difficult is a mystery. I pull up my social worker, Davina's, contact info and press the call button.

She answers right away. "Jasmine, how are things

going? I had you on my check-in calendar today but you beat me to it."

"Hey, Davina." I take a deep breath. "Things are okay. Pretty non-eventful for the most part."

"Well, non-eventful is good, I would think, all things considered." I can hear the smile in her voice. "How are you fitting in with your new family? Any concerns?"

"Nope," I lie. "Everyone's been... nice, I guess. We're all still trying to get to know one another."

There's no way I'm telling her about how I'm being bullied at school or how cold Charles has been to me. As much as I don't like my birth father, or that school, I will admit it's the best place for me to meet my goals of getting custody of Belle.

"I'm glad to hear it, Jazz. Now, since you called me, I'm guessing you've got something on your mind? Talk to me, honey."

"I was hoping you could give me Belle's address. I've tried calling her dad several times. He answered once and said it'd be okay if I stopped by, but he's been ghosting me since. I need to see her with my own eyes. Make sure she's okay."

Davina sighs. "Honey, you know I can't do that."

"But—"

"Hold on, now. I wasn't done. Like I was saying, I can't give you her address, but I can try to coordinate a sibling visit. My placement check-in with her is scheduled for next week. I can ask then."

"Thank you, Davina. I really appreciate it. I miss her so much."

"I'm sure she misses you too, honey. I'll get back to you as soon as I can, okay?"

I nod. "Okay. I'll talk to you later."

I end the call, discouraged I didn't get Belle's address, but I know Davina will do her best. I suppose that's all I can hope for right now.

chapter fourteen

JAZZ

By Monday morning, I'm on emotional overload. Every one of my attempts to contact Belle went unanswered. When Charles returned from his trip, I was expecting another scolding, but what I got instead was complete avoidance, confirming my suspicion he doesn't really give a fuck about me.

I'm getting to the point where I've accepted this is my new reality—a world without my mom or my sister. Living in a mansion filled with the most frigid, superficial people I've ever met. I'm surrounded by more people than I ever have been, yet I've never felt so lonely.

"Hey, you okay?" Ainsley asks, sliding into her

regular parking spot at school. "You've been really quiet."

Since our houses are in the same gated community, she's been driving me to school every morning. Frank still picks me up most afternoons since she goes straight to ballet, but it's nice to see her friendly face at the beginning of each day. I especially need it today.

I stare out the window, sucking in my emotions. "I'm good. Just tired. I didn't sleep very well last night." At least that last part wasn't a lie.

We exit her Lamborghini Huracan and meet at the back. Our first classes are in different buildings, so this is where we usually part.

She pulls me into a hug. "You look like you needed one of these."

I squeeze her back, trying my damnedest not to cry. "I do. Thank you."

She smiles. "I'll see you at lunch, okay?"

I nod. "Yep. See you then."

If I wasn't so inside my head, maybe I would've noticed the looks I was getting when I stepped inside Lincoln Hall. Heard the increased chatter and snickering at my expense. Peyton—who came back home yesterday—steps in front of me, blocking my path.

I raise my eyebrows. "Excuse me."

She laughs mockingly as Whitney and Imogen flank her. "There's no excuse for you. What you did was unforgivable."

Breaking her nose is unforgivable? After she started it? Dramatic much?

I try to step around them, but they shift their bodies, blocking my path. I hitch my backpack higher on my shoulder and cross my arms over my chest. Knowing what a stickler Headmaster Davis is for violence around here, I'm not afraid she'll try to hit me, but she *can* make me late for class if she doesn't move her ass.

"Move, Peyton. You've made your point."

Her icy blue eyes narrow into slits. "I don't think I have, but I will. Just give me time."

Before I can say another word, all three girls step aside to allow me through. I walk to my locker, wondering why the hell everyone is still standing around. Shouldn't they be getting to class? A few people make pathetic attempts to trip me, others fling insults. One guy even grabbed my ass, asking how much I charged for a hand job. I ignore them for the most part, until I reach the crowd gathered around my locker, waiting to witness my humiliation. They part as I approach, and that's when I see it.

In bright white spray paint, the word *whore* is written vertically, covering the entire length of the wooden door. I can tell from the shine and strong fumes that it's still wet which means someone must have just done this. I do my best not to react as I enter my combination and open it. As I'm grabbing my calculator off the top shelf, my hand brushes against a sheet of paper. My jaw drops as I pull it out and see the photo that's printed on it. Two guys and one girl are engaging in a threesome—or the prelude to it, anyway. My phone dings a moment later, so I dig it out of my bag and see that I have an Instagram alert.

Waiting in my DMs is a video clip and several photos from an obviously fake account. As I read the message that came with it, I feel like I'm going to vomit.

This went out to the entire student body ten minutes ago. Now they all know what a whore you truly are.

I turn around, scanning the area for the people I know are responsible for this. I don't think once I spot them; I simply charge over there and slam the piece of paper into Kingston's chest.

"What the fuck is this?" I seethe.

Kingston glances at the photo and flicks it to the ground. "It seems pretty self-explanatory to me."

"How did this happen? Who took these pictures?"

Bentley and Reed are standing on either side of him, their expressions not revealing anything.

Kingston shrugs. "Your guess is as good as mine. It seems as if Donovan Bradshaw's pool house has hidden security cameras. Someone must've leaked the footage."

"I don't believe you." I shake my head. "I don't even remember this. When did this happen?"

"Oh, new girl, you wound me." Bentley flattens his palm over his heart. "How can you forget the best dicking of your life?"

I glare at him. "I did not—" I lower my voice. "*There was no dicking.* I would remember if I had sex with you. Especially *both* of you."

Bentley raises an eyebrow. "Those photos indicate otherwise. Are you denying you're the girl in the video, telling us to take our shirts off? You couldn't get on our jocks fast enough, sweetheart."

I bite my tongue. There's definitely no denying that it's me in that video.

Kingston leans into my ear. "You know what I remember? I remember how fucking hot you looked choking on my cock." He pulls back and smirks. "Look, princess, I don't like having these pictures floating around any more than you do, but what's done is done. And as we told you Friday night, that was a one-time thing. You're not nearly a good enough lay to warrant a repeat."

A chorus of "oooohs" and "burn" roll through the crowd.

My eyes are filling with tears, but I refuse to let these assholes see me cry. "Fuck. You."

Kingston shakes his head. "Didn't I just say that wasn't going to happen?"

I raise my clenched fist, but Kingston sees it coming from a mile away and pushes me away. The laughter increases tenfold as I stumble backward and fall on my ass. I know I'm about to break down, so I get up, duck into the nearest bathroom, and lock myself in a stall. However many minutes later, the door to the girls' room opens and several people shuffle in. I hold my breath, not wanting to alert them to my presence.

"Oh my God, did you see her face?" A girl laughs. "Priceless!" She sounds like Peyton, but I'm not positive.

"The truth hurts," a second girl says. "I heard she wanted Reed to join in too, but he shot her down and just watched. I don't even know why Bentley or Kingston fucked her when they could've had us. She's not even that pretty and she's a total slut. Obviously."

"Oh, Whit, don't pretend you wouldn't fuck all three of them if given the chance," the first girl says. "I know I would." Yep, that's definitely Peyton.

"She's still a whore," Whitney huffs.

A third girl says, "She'll learn real fast not to fuck with us. If that cunt thinks she can break Peyton's nose, steal our men, and get away with it, she has another thing coming."

I try looking through the crack in the stall, wanting to identify the other girl, but like everything in this building, they're not your standard cheap metal. These are thick wood and go down to the floor. The gap around the edges is almost nonexistent. It has to be Imogen. Those three always seem to travel together.

"Anyway," Peyton continues. "At least the kings formally admitted to their mistake and shunned her. Now, no one will touch that reject. And by the time the royals are done messing with her, she'll wish she never

140

met any of us. If I'm lucky, she'll run away back to the streets and live with her pimp or something."

I already do regret meeting you assholes.

"I can't wait to see it all unfold. She won't even see us coming." I believe it was Whitney who said that.

That's what you dumb fucks think. A little harassment and spray paint won't scare me away. Not when I have so much on the line.

~

Ainsley and I are eating lunch in the library. My last two classes were so awful, I just needed a break from it all. Especially considering I have to sit by the three dickheads next period.

"Okay, walk me through this again." Ainsley takes a bite of her sandwich. Thankfully, the library has a little café, so we won't be hungry for the rest of the afternoon.

"I've already told you everything. You saw the pictures."

She shakes her head. "I'm so sorry I didn't see the alert before you went inside the building. I could've saved you all that embarrassment if my phone wasn't on silent."

"It's not your fault. I had to go to my locker eventually. I'm sure those vultures would've waited as long as they had to." I take a bite of my own sandwich, despite the fact that my gut is still churning.

Ainsley stares at me, biting her bottom lip in concentration. "Okay... I'm just going to say it. Those pictures—and especially the video—are pretty damning, Jazz. There's no way of denying that you're the girl they're with."

I thunk my head on the table with a groan. "I know."

"So you *did* have sex with them—Bentley and my brother at the same time. And you seriously don't remember any of it?"

I sit back up and shake my head. "I don't remember a damn thing. Do you think it's possible someone put something in my drink?"

Her eyes widen. "Like a roofie?"

I nod. "Yeah, or something like it."

Ainsley shakes her head. "I don't know, Jazz. I mean, it's possible, because there were so many people there, but I know my brother or Bentley wouldn't have done that. They don't need to drug a girl to get laid."

I sigh. "It just doesn't make sense. I know the pictures look bad, but I don't *feel* like I had sex that night. It's been awhile since I've done it. Don't you think I would've been sore, at least a little bit?"

Ainsley shrugs. "I have no idea. Have you ever done it with multiple guys at the same time? I mean, besides the other night?"

"No. No judgment, but that kind of thing just isn't my style."

She raises her eyebrows. "You seemed *really* into it."

"I blame the alcohol and my weakness for bad boys."

My shoulders lift. "With those two in particular... I don't know. There's just something about them. They're both assholes, and I can't stand them, but you'd have to be blind not to recognize how extraordinarily attractive they are. Kingston's dark and broody thing does it for me and Bentley can be really charming when he's not being an ass."

"When is Bentley *not* an ass?" Ainsley laughs. "What about Reed? Are you attracted to him?"

I shake my head. "He's hot, sure, but I don't feel any sort of chemistry with him like I do with the other two."

She takes that in for a moment. "Well... I don't think he'll give up any information, but I'll work on Kingston to see if I can find out what really happened. As for the rest of the assholes around here, you just have to give it time. This is high school—there's always some sort of drama waiting around the corner. As soon as some new scandal surfaces, they'll forget this whole thing ever happened."

As much as I'd like to believe her, I don't think it's going to be that easy. I suppose time will tell.

chapter fifteen

KINGSTON

"What the hell were you thinking?" Peyton screams.

I've been blowing her off all day, but she followed me home after school so I couldn't ignore her anymore. I'm sure as fuck not about to let her inside, so we're having this argument in my garage.

I give her a dry look. "We are not actually together so I don't understand what your problem is."

She glares at me. "We had an agreement that you would be *discreet*. First, I have to hear about you fooling around with Ariana Romero in a hot tub and the same night you have a *threesome* with that piece of trash?"

"You wanna talk about being discreet? You're not exactly keeping the fact that you're fucking Lucas Gale on the regular a secret. How do you think that makes me look?"

She folds her arms over her chest. "There isn't any

evidence of it floating around cyberspace. And you have no relation to him, so it's a completely different situation."

I wave my hand dismissively. "The pictures are gone —the account they came from was deleted."

Peyton rolls her eyes. "Yeah, *after* the entire student body saw it. Who knows how many screenshots are out there?"

I raise my eyebrows. "Your point?"

"Why can't it be me?" She throws her hands up. "If you want to fuck, *fuck me*!"

I've had enough of this bitch. I pin her to the side of my Range Rover with my hand on her neck. Peyton's spine bows, and her nipples harden beneath her uniform shirt. Fucking Christ, of course this would turn her on.

I squeeze harder. "Maybe if you weren't screwing around behind my back we would've never broken up in the first place."

Peyton and I were together for almost two years. I didn't love her, but I enjoyed fucking her and she didn't annoy me nearly as much as she does now. After I found out she'd been spreading her legs for half the football team during the last six months of our relationship, I cut her off. No bitch is going to fuck around behind my back and get away with it.

When I agreed to reconcile—at least as far as the general public was concerned—I made it clear I would *not* be a one-woman man this time around. She didn't like it, but she did accept it with one caveat. Once we got engaged, neither one of us would fuck someone else. Hopefully for me, that day will never come.

Peyton claws at my hand, panic now starting to set in. "I'm sorry!" She takes a deep breath when I loosen my grip. "If I truly thought you'd get as mad as you did, I would've never done it."

Yeah, right.

"I believe that just as much as I believe your tits grew three cup sizes during your summer in France."

She glares. "I didn't hear you complaining when you were fucking them."

I step back and pinch the bridge of my nose. "Peyton, can we not do this right now? Bentley and Reed will be here any minute. You need to leave."

Peyton pastes a smile on her face, as if the last five minutes never happened. "Sure, baby. I'm meeting the girls to go shopping anyway. Maybe I can suck you off later? You don't even need to touch me."

My jaw tics. If she thinks I'll allow her to mark her supposed territory, she's even dumber than I thought. "Not happening, Peyton. It's *never* happening."

She stomps her foot, all traces of a smile gone. "Well, if you think I'm going to just stand by and let you fuck my slutty stepsister, you're wrong!"

I scoff. "And why exactly do you think you have *any* say in the matter?"

"Because if you touch Jasmine again, our deal is off." Peyton looks pleased with herself, thinking she's

147

backed me into a corner. Little does she know I'm working on a backup plan where I won't need her anymore.

"Oh yeah?" I taunt. "Don't forget, you need me for something, too."

Peyton clenches her fists at her side. "Don't you dare dip your dick into that skank again, Kingston. If you do, we're going to have a big problem."

I fist her hair and pull back until she winces in pain. "You know I don't respond kindly to threats, so I'd recommend thinking twice before you start throwing any around. Are we clear?"

Tears prick at her eyes. "Yes."

I release her and give her a little shove. "Get the fuck out, Peyton, before I get really pissed. Who knows what I'll do to you if that happens."

She can't get away from me fast enough. Peyton knows what I'm capable of. A couple years back, I went through a self-destructive phase after discovering what my father and Callahan were up to. Before I decided to channel that rage into taking them down, I was an angry motherfucker. Scare tactics aside, I would never intentionally hurt a woman—I watched my father do it too many times in my life—but I did beat dozens of guys to a bloody pulp in an underground fighting ring.

As Peyton's Ferrari peels out of the driveway, Bent and Reed pull up.

I nod as they exit Reed's new DB 11. "'Sup?"

Both guys offer up a fist bump before we cut through the house to get to the back.

"Daddy Davenport around?" Bentley asks.

"Nah." I gesture for them to follow me. The pool house is off-limits to the staff unless I'm in school, so it's one of the only places I feel comfortable having this discussion.

When we get there, Reed switches on the big screen, tuning it to the NFL Network while Bent hooks his phone up to the speakers and starts blasting some Post Malone bullshit.

I open the fridge and toss a beer to each of them.

"Why was Little Miss Priss here?" Bentley asks. "I thought you shut that shit down a while ago."

"I did." I take a few gulps of beer. "That doesn't stop her from yapping my ear off every chance she gets though."

Reed barks out a laugh. "What's her problem now?"

"One guess." I flop on the couch and kick my feet up on the coffee table.

"Ah, jealous of Jazzy Jazz, is she?" He throws his head back and groans. "Goddamn, I cannot get that girl out of my mind."

Me neither.

I smack him upside the head. "Stop thinking with your dick, dumbass."

Reed laughs. "Oh, fuck off, Davenport. You're just as obsessed. Anyone who saw that video can plainly see how badly you *both* want her. That's why Peyton's

149

freaking out so much. Unfortunately for you assholes, painting that target on Jazz's back was a surefire way of ensuring that never happens."

I point to him. "You're not exactly an innocent party here."

He smirks. "Maybe not... but I don't want to fuck her."

"Only because you want to make sweet looove to her new bestie," Bentley taunts.

I punch his arm this time. "Shut the fuck up."

Bentley rubs his bicep. "What'd you do that for? It's not like it's not true!" He turns toward Reed. "Tell him, dude."

Reed holds his palms up. "I'm not saying shit." He nods to me. "So what's the deal with your dad and Callahan? Your guy get anything?"

I release a heavy breath. I hired a PI to dig around a little and so far, Charles and my dad look squeaky clean. They've been very careful not to leave a trail.

"Nothing useful. I need to get into Callahan's office. He has to be keeping records in there. I couldn't find shit at my house."

"How are you supposed to do that?" Bentley asks. "Whenever you're at Casa Callahan, Peyton's on your ass the entire time. Your only viable excuse to be in that house is to see her."

I smile when an idea springs to mind. "Not the *only* excuse."

Reed raises his brows. "Jazz?"

"Exactly. Before Peyton left, she mentioned she was going shopping, so she'll probably be gone for hours." I grab my keys off the table and stand. "No time like the present."

～

"Fuck."

I shift my car into park and pull the e-brake. My dad's car is parked in Callahan's circular driveway right in front of mine. I won't be able to sneak into his office, but since I'm already here, I might as well do some recon.

The house manager, Ms. Williams, answers the door when I ring the bell. "Mr. Davenport, I'm afraid Miss Peyton is out at the moment. Your father is in with Mr. Callahan. Are you here to see him?"

"No, I'm actually here to see Jasmine if she's available." I smile, laying on the charm. "We're in the same literature class and I wanted to talk to her about an assignment."

She steps aside, allowing me to enter. "Oh, please come in. I believe she's still in the gym. Do you know where that is?"

"I do. Thank you, Ms. Williams."

She nods. "Very well. Please let me know if you need anything."

Their gym is on the basement level, so I head downstairs, passing a theater room, the main game room, and another living room, before reaching my destination. I pause in the doorway as I spot Jasmine running on a treadmill. Goddamn. Her back is turned to me, so I have a perfect view of her heart-shaped ass running in tiny workout shorts. She has a set of Beats on her head, so she hasn't heard me enter the room. I take advantage of that and watch her for a while as she maintains an impressive pace. The back of her sports bra is drenched with sweat, so she must have been running for a while. Jasmine's caramel skin shines from the exertion, little beads dripping down her exposed spine. Her dark ponytail swings from side to side as she pumps her arms. Fuck, I'd love to wrap that hair around my fist as I fucked her from behind.

When my dick can't take it anymore, I step farther into the room so she can see me out of her peripheral.

Jasmine stumbles backward when she sees me. "Jesus shit!" She yanks the emergency stop button and steps off the belt. "What the hell are *you* doing here?"

I don't bother hiding the fact that I'm checking her out from head to toe. "I came to see you."

Her chest heaves while she tries regulating her breaths. My eyes are drawn to her perky little tits, remembering how those light brown nipples felt on the tip of my tongue.

She parks a hand on her hip. "I have nothing to say to you, so you can get the fuck out."

"You sure about that?" I step closer, smiling when

she retreats. I continue walking until she's pressed against the arm of the treadmill she just hopped off of.

"Yes, I'm sure!" Her chocolate eyes bounce between my lips and my eyes. "Leave, Kingston."

I reach out and tug her bottom lip from her teeth. "Is that what you really want?"

I press the full length of my body against hers so she can feel the hard-on I'm sporting. Fuck, what is it about this girl that makes my dick take the lead?

Her breath hitches. "Yes, that's what I really want." Jasmine's eyelids flutter when I run the bridge of my nose along her neck. She smells like vanilla and clean sweat and it makes me want to fucking devour her. "I can't believe you'd even have the nerve to show your face after what you did to me earlier today."

She shivers when I taste her salty skin. "I told you, I'm not the one who leaked it."

Jasmine flattens her palms on my chest and pushes me away. "And I told you, I don't believe you. Besides, what happened to, 'That was a one-time thing,'?" She lowers her voice on the last sentence, mocking me.

My lips curve. "That may not be exactly true. I'd be down for a repeat if you promise to keep quiet about it."

If I thought she was pissed before, that was nothing compared to the look she's giving me now.

"Keep quiet?" Jasmine shouts. If we weren't so far into the bowels of this giant house, I'd be concerned her volume would gain attention. "Are you fucking serious?" She pushes me again, which I allow. Let's be real; I easily have a hundred pounds on her—if I didn't want to move, I wouldn't be going anywhere. "Who the fuck do you think you are? You're delusional! You're so used to someone catering to your every whim, you have no idea what it's like to live in the real world! You can't just treat someone like shit and expect them to be okay with it! There are consequences for your actions! Where I come from, people could get murdered for disrespecting someone like you did to me. The world isn't always pretty or accommodating, but you have no fucking clue, because live in Fantasy Land."

"You have *no fucking clue* what *my* life is like, princess," I snap. "Trust me, I am *well aware* how ugly and unfair this world can be. I fucking live with the consequences *every goddamn day*." I cuff both of her wrists in my hand when she tries hitting me.

We're both panting. Seething. I feel like I'm going to implode if I don't find an outlet for this aggression. I release her wrists and take a step back, not trusting myself, but Jasmine fists the fabric of my shirt and pulls me back into her.

I frown. "What are you—"

"Shut. Up." Jasmine presses up on her toes, grips the back of my neck, and slams her lips against mine.

Our teeth clash and our tongues tangle in a frenzy of barely leashed violence. My cock jerks as she bites my bottom lip hard enough to draw blood before sucking the sting away. I lift her tiny body, hitching her legs around my waist, before backing her into the nearest wall.

"Fuck," I groan, grinding my dick into her core. "You drive me crazy."

Jasmine moans when I bite the fleshy part of her neck. "Likewise."

I hiss when she presses into me harder. I can feel the warmth from her pussy through my slacks as she slides her body up and down, stroking me.

"You keep that up, sweetheart, and you're going to get fucked."

She looks like she's actually considering it. Christ.

After a moment, Jazz slowly peels my hands off her thighs and drops to the ground. "Get out."

My body wars with my head. I know she wants me just as much as I want her. Her skin has the telltale flush of arousal, her nipples are hard, and her lips are slightly parted.

Jasmine's eyes narrow. "I mean it, Kingston. Get. The. Fuck. Out."

I hold up my hands. "Chill the fuck out. I'm leaving."

I duck into the theater room and throw myself into one of the plush recliners, waiting for my dick to calm down. I groan as I adjust myself. *What the fuck was that?* I've never—and I do mean *never*—let my dick control me before I met Jasmine. Thank fuck she had the sense to stop that train wreck before it had gone any further.

Because I sure as shit didn't.

chapter sixteen

JAZZ

I run a towel through my hair as I head into my closet to get dressed. As soon as I got home from school, I had so much pent up frustration from the day, I needed something to release it. Running has always been an outlet for me and since I'm not too familiar with the area yet, I figured I'd make use of the expansive home gym. Of course Charles Callahan has nothing but the best equipment. It took me a while to figure how to even turn the damn treadmill on, but once I did, it was pretty easy to select a pre-programmed course.

About four miles into my run, I reached that place in my head where all I focused on was the burn in my muscles. What my body was capable of. It's a blissful space where whatever you have going on in your life, doesn't matter. Right as I was feeling a sense of much needed peace, Kingston showed up, making me instantly irate. And aroused.

What is it about him I can't resist?

Yeah, he's probably the hottest guy I've ever met, but he's also an elitist asshole. A bully. Something inside of me tells me there's more though. That if I looked hard enough, I'd find the real reason he acts this way. I saw a flicker of pain when he was going off on me about living with consequences. Consequences of *what*, is what I'd like to know. Ainsley mentioned their mom died when they were eight. Is he still hurting from that, almost ten years later, or is it something more recent?

I shouldn't give a rat's ass about him, but I want to know what makes him tick. I feel like I *need* to know. As I'm braiding my wet hair, I catch sight of something outside my bedroom window.

What the hell?

My room faces the front of the house, so I have a direct view of the circular driveway. The same driveway where Kingston's car is currently parked. What is he still doing here? It's been almost an hour since I told him to leave.

I step out of my room and decide to investigate. I cover the entire basement level since that's last where I saw him, but he's nowhere to be found. Same thing for the main level. He must be in Peyton's room which bothers me a lot more than I'd like to admit. After seeing how they interact with one another, I have no doubt he's being honest when he says they're not together, but that doesn't mean they don't still have something physical going on, despite his barbs at dinner last week. Hell, for all I know, he was so worked up from our make-out sesh, he decided to use her to finish the job. She's made her willingness on that end quite apparent and Kingston's morals seem loose at best.

Right before I'm about to head back to my room, I spot him slinking toward Sperm Donor's end of the house.

What is he up to?

I silently trail behind Kingston, careful to look out for any staff members that could ruin my stealth. Kingston ducks into an alcove right outside my father's study. When I reach him, he doesn't look surprised in the least, as if he knew I was following him.

"What are—" I start to say.

I squeal when he bands his arms around my torso and slams a hand over my mouth, muffling my protests.

"Shut. Up," he growls into my ear. "Trust me when I say neither one of us want to be caught here right now."

The door to Charles' office is only about five feet away. I can hear quiet murmurs, but I can't make out anything clearly.

I squirm in his arms, trying to ignore the growing erection at my back.

Kingston tightens his hold. "Stop moving, goddammit. Are you trying to give me blue balls? *Again?*" I immediately halt all movement. "Now, if I let you go, do you promise not to say a word?"

I nod in agreement and gasp for air when he removes his hand from my mouth.

He holds a finger over his lips, telling me to be quiet as he creeps closer to the study. We're right outside the door before I can make out any words.

"—think she knows?"

"I doubt it," Charles answers. "I'm fairly certain her attitude is pure teenage rebellion but I'm keeping a close eye on it just in case."

Kingston slowly shakes his head when he sees the questions bubbling beneath my lips.

"She looks just like her mother," Preston says. "*Exactly* fucking like her. She was about the same age when you brought her in, right?"

"Yes," my father answers. "Only about two months difference. The resemblance is... disconcerting, considering she's my goddamn daughter. I may like 'em young, but even I have limits."

"Well, she's not *my* daughter so I'm not disturbed by it in the least." Kingston's dad laughs.

Wait... what? Kingston's eyes widen in warning when he sees my shock. Are they talking about me?

And my mother? Peyton looks a lot like Madeline, but I am a perfect replica of my teenage mother.

"Too bad you knocked her mom up in the first goddamn month," Preston muses. "She would have been in high demand."

High demand for what?

"I know." The stench of cigar smoke seeps through the crack at the bottom of the door before Charles speaks again. "If I recall correctly, it could've just as easily happened to you. You weren't exactly careful about wrapping it either, and your wife was pregnant with twins at the time."

"What can I say? She was pretty goddamn irresistible. So beautiful. Young. Naïve. Just how I like 'em." Kingston's jaw clenches as his dad belts out a boisterous laugh. "I still can't believe you didn't force her to get rid of it and you gave her a fucking legitimate job on top of it."

My father laughs. "Mahalia was certainly something special. Besides, once the kid came into play, she was twice as desperate and ready to please. We got a lot of good miles out of her between the two of us."

Well, that squashes any possibility they were talking about an unknown third daughter. I still don't know *what* the fuck they're talking about though. Well, besides the fact that both men apparently had sex with my mother. I swallow back bile at the thought.

"I remember," Preston says fondly. "Hell, if Jennifer

would've gone for it, I would've given her a nanny job. Damn woman insisted we didn't need one."

Kingston's fists are clenching so tightly, his knuckles are turning white.

"Well," Preston begins. "This trip down memory lane has been fun but I need to get going. I have a conference call with one of my suppliers in less than an hour."

Kingston grabs my hand and forcefully yanks me down the hall and into a guest bathroom. We listen as our fathers say goodbye to one another and wait a moment for his dad to leave. Once it's safe, he drags me out of the bathroom.

"Your bedroom. Now."

"What?" I have to speed walk to keep up with him. "What's going on?"

"Just shut up until we get to your room."

I want to tell him to fuck off but I'm more curious about what the hell we just heard so I follow. Once we're safely behind a locked door, Kingston turns on the Bluetooth speaker I have on my desk and presses buttons on his phone until "The Drug in Me is You" by Falling in Reverse starts playing.

He starts pacing in a circle. "You cannot repeat a word of what you just heard."

I take a seat on the edge of my bed. "I don't even know *what* the hell I just heard."

His angular jaw tics. "It's better if it stays that way."

"What does that—" I gasp when it hits me. "Holy

shit, you *do* know what they were talking about, don't you?"

Kingston runs his hands over his head until his hair is standing on end. "Jasmine, I'm fucking serious. *Don't* dig into this and don't tell *anyone* about it."

"They were talking about my mom! I have every right to know why. And why are you not freaking out about the fact that your dad apparently had an affair with my mom? It sounded like our fathers were both sleeping with her at the same time. That's just... *gross*. And so unlike the woman I knew."

He stops pacing and closes the gap between us. I'm on my back with him hovering over me before he stops. I don't miss the semi pressing into my thigh.

His hand wraps around my neck, but he doesn't put any pressure on it. "I know your brain is running a mile a minute right now, but you have no idea what you're dealing with."

We both groan as he positions his hardness between my thighs and drops his weight on me. I'm wearing a pair of thin joggers, so I feel every inch of him as he rubs himself against my clit, growing bigger with each slide.

"Kingston," I pant. "Quit trying to distract me. I need answers."

He lifts his face from my neck and straightens his arms into a plank position. "I know. And I'll give them to you when the time is right." He puts his hand over my mouth when I try to speak. "Jazz, I give you my word. I know you have no reason to trust me, but I need you to do it anyway. If you go running your mouth, you'll put yourself in danger. Our fathers are not good men. They've done some really fucked up shit and you *do not* want to be on their radar."

My eyes widen. He's right; I have absolutely no reason to trust him. But the conviction in his voice, the fact that he actually looks scared right now, tells me I can. At least about this.

He moves his hand away from my mouth when I nod. "Okay."

Kingston searches my eyes. "Okay?"

"Yes." I push on his chest until he gets off me. "But I won't wait forever."

"That's fair." He pulls his phone out of his pocket and runs his thumbs over the screen. When he's done, my phone chimes with a text alert. How did he get my number? "I need to go. You have my number if you need to reach me. I'll see you in the morning."

I grab my phone after he leaves and check the messages. Sure enough, there's a new message from an unknown number.

Unknown: Don't be stupid. Keep your mouth shut.

I program his name into my phone and send a quick reply.

Me: *middle finger emoji*

I open my window as he approaches his car.

Kingston pulls his phone out of his pocket and checks the screen.

He looks up in my direction after reading the message. I can't be sure from this distance, but I swear he just winked before getting in his car and driving away.

What the fuck did I just walk into?

~

When I step outside to meet Ainsley the next morning, she's nowhere to be found. Instead, a matte black wet dream of a car is parked directly up front with a stupidly sexy guy leaning against it.

"What are you doing here?"

Kingston flashes a predatory grin. "Giving you a ride to school."

I shake my head vehemently. "Nuh-uh. You must have me confused with Peyton."

He takes his time perusing my body from head to toe before replying. "Trust me, sweetheart, I could *never* confuse you for Peyton."

I ignore what that look does to my panties and pull out my phone to text Ainsley.

"Don't bother," Kingston says. "Ainsley's car is getting detailed. Reed's giving her a lift and I told her I'd pick you up."

I stuff my phone in my backpack. "Why couldn't *you*

drive her since you live together? I'll just ask Frank to drive me."

"Because I wanted *you* to ride with me, not my sister. And tough luck, sweetheart, but Frank has the day off."

I sigh, realizing I'm not going to win this argument. "How do you know that?"

A devilish grin lights up his face. "I have my sources."

Kingston opens the weird ass door. It hinges forward until the entire thing is vertical above the ground. "Get in the car, princess."

"I'd rather walk."

That's a total lie. I *really* want to ride in that car, but a girl's gotta have some pride.

He gives me a wry look. "You'd rather walk *ten miles?*"

I prop a hand on my hip. "Maybe I don't trust you behind the wheel of that thing."

Kingston lovingly caresses the top of the vehicle. "That *thing*, is a Koenigsegg Agera RS. She's a two-point-five-million dollar piece of performance machinery that can go from zero to sixty in two-point-nine seconds. Watch how you speak about her. You don't want to hurt her feelings."

My jaw drops. I can't fathom paying that much money for a car. "Wow... you give new meaning to the word spoiled. Your dad must love you *a lot*."

He narrows his eyes. "Actually, it was an eighteenth birthday present to myself." Kingston grabs my hand and pulls me into him before whispering. "For the record, I wouldn't take *shit* from that bastard. Not that I need to explain myself to you, but my mother left me a considerable inheritance. It's old family money from her side. I get everything on my twenty-first birthday, but the trustee made an exception to release the funds to buy this. Two mill is *nothing* compared to what I have left."

I pull away from him, suppressing a shiver from having his hot breath in my ear. "Is that supposed to impress me, rich boy?"

Kingston smirks. "Nah. I know it *doesn't* impress you which is why I told you. It's not exactly something I go around bragging about. I'm not a moron—that'd be asking for trouble. This trust thing goes both ways, Jazz."

Shit. I have nothing to say to that.

He laughs. "You're going to make us late if you don't get your ass in the car. Now *get in the damn car.*"

I hate how my body responds to his commanding tone.

"Fine," I huff. "But I'm finding my own way home."

As he's closing my door he says, "You keep telling yourself that, sweetheart."

Kingston rounds the front of the vehicle and gets in on the driver's side.

Fuck, the whole car smells like leather and his spicy

cologne. It's doing all sorts of things to my girly parts, and I hate him for it.

He presses a button to start the engine and fastens his seat belt. "You ready?"

I hold my backpack on my lap as a shield. "Just drive the fucking car. The sooner I can get out of this thing, the better."

I can't resist smiling when he releases a deep belly laugh.

Kingston revs the engine. "Hold on, sweetheart."

I'm glued to my seat as soon as Kingston starts driving, navigating the hills and curves in the road like a pro. I never dreamed I'd be sitting in a fine piece of machinery like this. The interior is matte black as well —save for the chrome center console—with subtle orange trim. I was never into flashy cars, but sitting in this one, feeling the power behind it, I can certainly see the appeal. I squeeze my thighs together as the throaty rumble of the engine causes my seat to vibrate. Thank God I'm wearing my school blazer because I'm pretty sure my nipples are hard right now. Fuck, this thing is sex on wheels.

Kingston gives me a knowing grin when I bite my lip to stifle a moan. "You doing okay over there, princess? You look flushed."

I roll my eyes as the car hugs the pavement around another tight corner. "Fuck off, Davenport. Just because I happen to like the car doesn't mean the driver is nearly as appealing."

His cocky smirk tells me he knows that's total bull-shit. "You keep telling yourself that, sweetheart."

I stare straight ahead, tuning him out for the remainder of the short drive. I sigh in relief as we pull through the gates of Windsor Academy, knowing I'll be out of this sexy as fuck car that smells even sexier because Kingston's cologne permeates the air. My reprieve is short-lived though as I notice all eyes on us as we slowly make our way to a parking spot. I sink lower in my seat, wanting to crawl into a hole and hide. Why didn't I think of this earlier? I should've had him drop me off right outside of the school grounds.

I groan.

Kingston pulls the car to a stop and glances my way. "Something wrong?"

"This is not going to go well."

"Relax, Jazz. I just gave you a ride. No big deal."

"Easy for you to say." I cringe when I see Peyton approaching the car. "I can guarantee Peyton will think it's a *very* big deal."

He scoffs. "Peyton can go fuck herself."

I shake my head as I open the door. "Might as well get this over with."

The moment I step out of the car, shocked gasps and chatter spreads throughout the parking lot.

"What the hell is this?" Peyton shrieks.

"Calm your tits, Peyton," Kingston growls.

"What the fuck do you think you're doing?" she

screams. "Don't tell me to calm down when I see that skank step out of your car!"

Kingston hits a button on his key fob, locking the vehicle. He takes a page from Reed's book and stands there looking bored out of his mind. "Don't act like you own me, Peyton. You are *nothing* to me. *We* are nothing."

Cue even more gasps and chatter.

The crowd's attention has now fully shifted to them, so I take the opportunity to escape while I can. My eyes are trained on the pavement as I head toward the main building where my first class is held. Just as I think I'll actually make it unscathed, Kingston shouts my name.

I freeze and look over my shoulder. "What?"

The asshole actually winks. "I'll see you at lunch."

Aaaaaannd now everyone's attention is back on me. I hear the fucker laugh as I flip him off on my way into the building.

chapter seventeen

KINGSTON

This new plan of mine is going even better than I thought. After what happened last night, I decided I need to keep a close eye on Jasmine to ensure she doesn't go snooping around. The only feasible way I can see myself doing that is to switch gears and use this crazy chemistry we have as leverage. I can tell she's too smart to rely solely on that, so I need to bring her in a little, allow her to see a side of me that very few people get. If I can get her to actually *like* me, I think she'll be a lot easier to control. And if I can convince her to fuck me in the process, even better.

First, I had to deal with the Peyton situation, which she made nice and easy by flipping her shit in front of half the student body. By the end of first period, word will spread to the other half. I knew Jazz would never fully be on board if Peyton and I were still together, even if it was strictly for appearances. Now, not only will the entire student body know Peyton and I broke up, rumors will fly about me and Jasmine. People will speculate as to whether or not their supposed king has taken an interest in the new girl.

Bentley and Reed approach me as the crowd of gawkers finally disperse.

Bentley's lips curve into a grin. "You wanna tell me what that was about?"

I motion for them to walk with me so we're not late for our first class. "Change of plans."

"What exactly happened between you and Jazzy Jazz last night?" Bentley wiggles his brows. "You tap that?"

I roll my eyes. "No, dumbass. Not yet anyway."

"So that means she's still fair game?"

I shrug, trying to mask my annoyance. "Even if I *had* fucked her, she'd still be fair game. It's not like I actually give a shit. She's just a means to an end."

Maybe if I keep telling myself that, I'll believe it.

Reed laughs. "Right. You think we're that stupid? We know you better than anyone, man. Drop the bullshit."

"It's not bullshit." I slap Bentley on the back, maybe a little harder than necessary. "You wanna hit it, be my guest. Just don't get in my way if I do, too. I need her to trust me for this to work."

Reed frowns. "How would banging her accomplish that?"

I scoff. "Please. We all know chicks can't have sex without emotion, no matter how vehemently they deny it. If Jazz feels some sort of emotional attachment to me—*any* sort of attachment, really—she'll be much more willing to trust me. More importantly, she won't get in my way. If I need to feed her the D to make that happen, so be it. It's not exactly a hardship."

Bentley fist bumps me. "Hells yeah! Operation Bang New Girl is officially on!"

Reed shakes his head. "I hope you know what you're doing, man."

Yeah, me too, buddy. Me too.

～

By the time lunch rolls around, things are still running smoothly. All conversation ceases when the guys and I walk into the dining room. We had already discussed it, so Reed and Bentley aren't surprised in the least when I bypass our usual table, but the rest of the room is, including Peyton and her bitch squad. I hear all three of them audibly gasp when Bentley and I pull out the chairs on either side of Jasmine and Reed takes the one next to my sister.

Jasmine is equally shocked, staring at me with an open mouth. I fight the urge to press my lips against hers and instead, place my index finger under her chin, gently pushing up until her mouth closes.

"Didn't want you to start drooling, princess."

My teeth grind together when Bentley pulls her into his side and kisses her on the cheek. "Hey, Jazzy Jazz. Whatcha having for lunch?"

She pushes him away. "What does it matter? And what are you doing here?"

"I'm with Jazz," my sister says. "What the hell are you guys up to? Why aren't you sitting with the other royals?"

Reed smirks when she uses air quotes accompanied by an eye roll on that last word.

Bentley bumps his shoulder into Jasmine's. "I wanted to be by you, baby."

She shakes her head and looks at Reed expectantly.

He shrugs. "I don't give a fuck where I sit as long as I have food in front of me."

Reed and Ainsley exchange a loaded glance. I make a note to ask him about it later.

Jazz narrows her gaze on me. "What about you?"

"I felt like eating here." I raise an eyebrow. "Anyone got a problem with that?"

She glances over at our normal table and sees three sets of false-lashed eyes glaring a hole through her. Yep, *they* definitely have a problem with it. My lips twitch when Jazz raises an eyebrow in challenge, which only incenses them further.

She turns back to me. "Fine. You can stay. But only because I know it drives those fake bitches crazy."

I offer her a wry look. "How magnanimous of you."

She shrugs. "I try."

The five of us dig into our food. The guys and I grabbed steak and potatoes, Ainsley got a California roll, and Jazz selected the cheeseburger on an artisan bun with truffle fries. That's one thing I've noticed about her—she doesn't eat rabbit food like most chicks in this school. The girl has one of the tightest bodies I've ever seen—I have no idea where it all goes. She must run *a lot*.

"Jazz, what are you doing this afternoon?" Ainsley asks. "Wanna watch my rehearsal and we can grab a bite to eat after?"

She nods. "Sure."

My twin is starring in her ballet studio's production of Cinderella. Dancing is her life—she's been taking classes four days a week for the last ten years or so. After our mom died, I think it started out as her way of coping, but it turned into something she actually loves. So much so, she wants to attend Juilliard and dance professionally after graduation. I personally don't understand her fascination with it, but I'm glad she has something to focus on. Plus, it gets her out of the house a lot which is a good thing. I don't want her around our father any more than she needs to be.

Ainsley beams. "Great! I can give you a ride home to change then we can—"

"She has plans," I interrupt. "With me."

Jasmine folds her arms across her chest. "I sure as hell do *not*."

My eyes drill into hers. "You *do*."

177

She scoffs. "And what plans would those be?"

My smile is promising all sorts of wicked things. "It's a surprise."

Ainsley's eyes bounce back and forth between us. "Uh... what am I missing here? What's going on between you two?" She turns to me. "And not that I'm complaining, but what's up with you dumping Peyton's ass in the parking lot this morning? It's practically all anyone is talking about."

Bentley laughs while Reed continues inhaling his food. Meanwhile, Jazz and I are locked in a silent battle.

She glances in my sister's direction. "Absolutely *nothing* is going on between us."

"That's our business—not yours," I say at the same time.

Ainsley holds her palms up. "O-kay then. Don't worry about it, Jazz. We can always do it another day. You two have fun doing whatever secret shit you have planned."

I smile victoriously while Jazz's face flushes in anger. "Meet me out front after the final bell. I'll take you home to change then we can be on our way."

She shakes her head. "I'm sorry, but when exactly did you become the boss of me?"

I lean into her ear, nuzzling my nose against the lobe. "Don't test me, Jazz. One way or the other, you're *coming* with me."

"Fine. But you're feeding me."

"Oh, I'll feed you something real good, baby. I'll give you a hint. It starts with D and rhymes with stick."

She shivers. "I meant actual food, asshole."

I pull back with a smile. "I suppose I can do that too."

Bentley looks between us. "Can I get in on this party?"

"No!" both Jasmine and I say in unison.

"I need better friends," Bent pouts. "At least I still have Reed to entertain me."

"Nope," Reed says through a bite of his baked potato. "I have plans."

Bentley frowns. "Doing what?"

Reed shrugs. "Just stuff."

I narrow my eyes when both he and my sister suddenly become awfully fascinated with the table. I know he has the hots for Ains but I've already made it crystal clear she's off-limits. Reed's a good guy—one of the best I know—but he hasn't been very discriminating with his dick since he lost his virginity at fifteen. My sister doesn't need to get mixed up in that shit.

"What kind of stuff?" I ask.

"Go to the mall," he answers. "I have to find a birthday present for my mom, so I'll probably drop in that damn purse store she like. Maybe check out the new LeBrons while I'm there. Stuff like that."

There's something he's omitting, but I'm dropping

it for now because I have to make a few calls before I have to get back to class.

"I'm out. I've got some arrangements to make before lunch is over." Just for shits and giggles, I place a kiss on Jazz's cheek as I stand. She stiffens as I expected, and out of the corner of my eye, I can see Peyton fuming. "I'll see you in Lit, babe."

I have to bite back my laughter as I feel Jasmine glaring at me while I walk out of the room. Who knew fucking with her would be so much fun?

chapter eighteen

JAZZ

It seems as if the kingdom is rallying behind their queens. By the time lunch rolled around, I'd been subjected to countless taunts, trip attempts, insults, and shoulder checks. For whatever reason, all the guys are staying as far away from me as possible, but there's plenty of female students to pick up the slack. I almost texted Ainsley, asking her to meet me in the library for lunch, but then I realized that would make them think they're winning and I refused to do that.

I will admit I got a little thrill when the guys sat down at our table, knowing how much it bothered Peyton. I know it's petty, but after the morning I'd had, I don't feel bad about it. Unfortunately, Kingston's little stunt only made the catty behavior even worse for the second half of the day, but it was almost worth it to see the look on my evil stepsister's face.

Speaking of Kingston... my phone buzzes with a text from him, indicating he's waiting for me out front. He dropped me off after school so I could change, and he went home to do the same. He said to dress casual and comfortable so I'm wearing a pair of skinny jeans, a plain red t-shirt, and my favorite pair of Chucks. Thankfully, neither Madeline or my father are home— no surprise there. They would both probably shit a brick if they saw me leaving the house in this outfit. I don't understand what their problem is with the minimal wardrobe I brought with me, but they've made their distaste abundantly clear. Sure, everything besides underwear were bought at a thrift shop, but they're all in good condition. It's not like I'm walking around in anything faded or stained. Maybe they would approve if I called it vintage instead of second hand. I snort at the thought.

I take one last glance in the mirror before walking out the door, smoothing out a few stray hairs from my ponytail. *What am I doing?* This is Kingston Davenport —asshole extraordinaire. I shouldn't try looking good for him. Hell, I shouldn't even be going anywhere with him, but I have to admit, I'm curious to see where he's taking me. As intimidating as he seemed at first, I don't think he would ever physically hurt me. Ainsley loves him too much for him to be *that* kind of guy. But I do think he's capable of some major psychological damage which is why I need to keep my guard up. I need to remind myself this is an information gathering mission. My stupid hormones need to take a hike and quit compelling me to want him.

Kingston knows something about my mother. Something big, I'm guessing. And I need to know what that is, so here we go. I step outside and see a shiny white Range Rover parked in front of the door. Kingston's behind the wheel and he pops the locks when I approach the passenger side.

I climb into the tan leather interior that still bears that new car smell. "Where's your car?"

Kingston's Ray-Bans slide down the bridge of his nose. "This *is* my car."

I roll my eyes. "I meant the fancy black one. How many cars do you own anyway?"

He flashes a wicked smile. "I have this, the Agera, and a Ducati."

I fasten my seat belt and mumble, "Ah, the lifestyles of the rich and infamous."

I must not have been quiet enough because Kingston laughs. "I like nice vehicles. Sue me."

I glance around the cabin as he pulls out of the driveway and spot a booster seat in the back. "Uh... why do you have a booster seat? I know you don't have any other siblings. Is there a Davenport love child I don't know about?"

Kingston scowls. "Probably more than one." When my eyes widen, he adds, "But not one of mine."

My lips form into an O when understanding dawns. "Oh."

I don't have anything to say to that. It's obviously a touchy subject for him, so I drop it.

"Are you going to tell me where we're going?"

"You'll see." He pulls onto the main road and turns up the music.

I bob my head along to Drake's latest album while Kingston drives. As we pull onto the freeway heading south, I run through a list of places he could be taking me. The possibilities become slimmer and slimmer as we pass through LA. I'm confused as fuck when he takes a South Central exit. This is where I grew up—I know these streets well. We're maybe three miles from my old apartment. What I don't know, is why we're here.

"Kingston, what's going on?"

He turns off the main road into a neighborhood. "Almost there."

"Almost *where?*"

Kingston pulls up to the curb in front of a small Spanish style home. "Stay here for a sec."

I watch as he steps through a metal gate and begins walking toward a man sitting on the front stoop, the brim of his hat pulled low as he smokes a cigarette. The white paint on the iron fence is a little worn, but the yard is well-kept and the paint on the stucco siding seems fairly fresh. Looking around, the entire street is that way for the most part.

Kingston shakes hands with the man and turns around, gesturing for me to join him. I exit the vehicle, still wondering what the hell is going on, when Kingston steps to the side a little, giving me a good look at the guy he was talking to.

"Holy shit."

Belle's father, Jerome, gives me a smarmy smile as I approach. "Well, look at you, Jasmine. Got yourself a rich boyfriend, huh? If I would've known that, I would've answered your calls."

I glare as he laughs. "Jerome." I glance over at Kingston. "What's going on?"

Kingston's eyes turn to Jerome and his fists clench when he sees the man giving me an obvious once-over. Jerome developed this leering habit of his about two years ago and it creeps me the fuck out. No middle-aged man should look at a teenager like that. "We need to get going," Kingston grits out. "Are you going to hold up your end of the bargain?"

Jerome crushes his cigarette beneath his sneakers and holds his palms out. "All right, no catching up then. Hold up a sec."

Hope blossoms as Jerome steps inside the house and calls my sister's name. I have so many questions running through my brain right now, but the only thing I can do is watch the door like a hawk, waiting for my favorite little person to step out of it.

Belle squeals when she sees me. "Jazz!"

Her tiny body leaps off the stoop and runs straight for me. I crouch down, my eyes filling with tears as I swoop her into my arms.

After a big squeeze, I pull back to look at her. It's been less than two months since we've seen each other, but it feels like two years. She seems so much older. The adorable fat on her cheeks has lost its fullness and she's missing another baby tooth.

"Hi, honey. I've missed you so much." I tug on one of her braids. "You look so pretty. Did you just get your hair done?"

Belle nods enthusiastically. "Uh huh. Daddy's girl-friend did 'em for me before bed last night. She said she was gonna bring home some pink and green beads after work tonight! She only had purple and I told her they *hafta* be pink and green."

I smile. Pink is Belle's favorite color and green is mine, so she always insisted on the same colored beads. She has her father's thick, coily hair which I adore in its natural state, but it's difficult for her to manage. Every six weeks or so, I'd braid and bead her hair while we watched Saturday morning cartoons and ate donut holes. Our mom was often working, so it became our special sister bonding time. I never realized how much I took that for granted until now.

Belle notices Kingston and wrinkles her little nose. "Who's the boy?"

I'm about to answer when Kingston crouches down to her level and takes her hand in his. "I'm Kingston. Jazz is my friend."

Belle giggles. "Are you her *boy*friend?"

He laughs. "No. Not her boyfriend. Not yet,

anyway." He winks. "Maybe you could put in a good word for me."

She narrows her big chocolate eyes, making me smile. My sister is the sweetest girl, but she definitely has a layer of sass that comes out on occasion. "I don't know... what's your favorite kind of ice cream?"

Kingston rubs his chin in mock contemplation. "Hmm... it's probably a tie between mint chocolate chip or cookie dough."

Belle thinks about that for a moment. "Okay."

He raises an eyebrow. "Okay? Does that mean I pass the test?"

She nods. "Yep. Her other boyfriend didn't even like ice cream. He's dumb."

Kingston and I both laugh. God, this moment seems so surreal. Not only do I get to see my sister, but I'm seeing an entirely different side to Kingston. If someone would've told me an hour ago he is an absolute natural with children, I would've told them they were crazy.

Jerome opens the screen door and pokes his head out. "She goes to bed at eight so you need to bring her home by seven-thirty."

Kingston nods. "We'll be back by then."

Wait... what?

"We get to take her?"

"I'll explain later," he says. Kingston stands up and starts walking toward the car. When he gets there, he opens the rear door. Now the booster seat makes sense.

I grab Belle's hand and lead her to the Range Rover. "C'mon, sweetheart. Let's go."

I get her buckled in properly then I slide into the back with her. Now that I finally have her, I can't bear to be apart, even if it's only in the front seat.

Kingston doesn't question me as he gets behind the wheel and presses the ignition button. Belle is chatting animatedly, telling me about her new school, a few friends she made, her dad's girlfriend, who she says she likes a lot. She seems to be handling having her entire life uprooted much better than I have. It amazes me how resilient kids are.

I don't even pay attention to where we're going. I'm so absorbed by the fact that my sister is sitting right next to me, that I tune everything else out. It's not until Kingston pulls into a parking lot that I take a look around.

Oh my God.

Belle squeals when she sees the familiar landmarks. "Ooh! Can we get ice cream? And a pretzel? And ride in the shark heads?"

Kingston's eyes meet mine before he faces her. "Whatever you want, kiddo. This is your day."

I'm speechless as I help Belle out of the car.

He takes my hand. "This okay?"

I squeeze his hand, nodding. "It's more than okay."

His face lights up in a smile. "Let's go then. We only have a couple hours."

The three of us walk out of the public parking lot

hand-in-hand and climb the stairs leading to the pier. We weave through the crowd, making our way past souvenir and various food stands. As we pass through the entrance to Pacific Park, I glance up at the metal octopus above my head and recall the last time I was here. It was almost a year ago—my seventeenth birthday, to be exact. Belle and I were standing with our mom in this very spot. When Belle was a little younger, she was afraid to pass through the entrance because she thought the octopus was real and that it would swoop down and grab us with its tentacles if we went under it. Once we finally managed to convince her it was a sculpture, she'd stick her tongue out and say—

Belle tugs on my hand to stop and sticks her tongue out. "I'm not afraid of you, fake octopus."

I'm practically on the verge of tears from the bittersweet memory. Kingston looks at me questionably and I mouth the same words to him that he said to me: *I'll tell you later.*

He nods, intuitively knowing how hard this is for me, but also how unbelievably happy I am. Could he possibly know what significance this place holds? He must, I decide. Kingston is obviously resourceful, not only finding out where my sister lives, but also making arrangements with her father, somehow convincing him to allow us to take her out for the afternoon. Why would this guy—one who's proven to be self-serving since the day we met—go out of his way to do something so incredibly selfless and sweet? This is by far, the nicest thing anyone has ever done for me.

I keep my questions to myself for now and decide to enjoy the limited time I have with Belle. We walk throughout the park and play some of the boardwalk games. Kingston shows off his baller skills, winning a giant stuffed animal for Belle by sinking some baskets. We go on the shark head tilt-a-whirl ride that always makes me feel sick, but Belle loves it so much, I suffer through it. We gorge on soft pretzels, churros, and cotton candy, before grabbing burgers for dinner. We even go for a ride on the Ferris wheel, and I somehow manage to make it through without crying. Grabbing a few ice cream cones, we eat them while walking on the beach as the sun begins to set.

Belle falls asleep on the ride home and remains asleep as I pull her out of the Range Rover. She wakes briefly when I kiss her on the forehead before handing her over to her dad. Kingston and Jerome exchange a few quiet words before Jerome takes my sister inside and we head back to the car.

I lean my head against the window as we pull onto the road and start driving. When we stop at a red light, Kingston places his hand on the side of my face. I turn into his palm, pressing a soft kiss in the middle before looking up.

"Thank you." My voice is barely above a whisper, but I know he hears me.

He swallows hard as his eyes search mine. The light

turns green, so he turns his attention back to the road, breaking the spell. I return my focus back to the window when he doesn't respond.

I startle when he links his fingers with mine a moment later. "Thank *you* for allowing me to be a part of it."

I squeeze his hand and smile. For the first time in months, I feel genuinely happy and it's all because Kingston Davenport does actually have a soul, and a damn fine one at that. Who would've thought?

chapter nineteen

KINGSTON

"So... Jasmine... Belle... I'm sensing a theme."

Jazz's smile grows. She hasn't stopped smiling all afternoon. I wouldn't think it was possible, but she's even more beautiful when she does that.

"Yeah, my mom had a thing for Disney princesses. Obviously." She laughs. "Jasmine was her favorite princess. According to her, she took one look at me, and knew that I would be independent and a little rebellious, but also sweet and compassionate. All traits someone would use to describe my royal counterpart."

Also a perfect way to describe you.

"For Belle," she continues. "That was actually *my* favorite princess, which is how she got her name, but she's actually lived up to it which is a little freaky when I think about it. My Belle is kind, imaginative, a little quirky, and the girl can spend hours in front of a book. We've spent a lot of time in the library."

"She's a pretty great kid."

"She's the best." Jazz sighs before turning her gaze to me. "Can I ask you something?"

"You can ask...can't guarantee I'll answer."

She shakes her head as she chuckles lightly. "How did you know? How did you find her?"

"You'd be surprised how easily you can gather information on anything or anyone with enough money and the right connections."

Having a private investigator at your beck and call doesn't hurt either.

"God, our childhoods have been so different. I can't fathom how easy things must have been for you."

My jaw clenches. "Just because I have money, doesn't mean I've had it easy."

She looks away. "You're right; I'm sorry. That was an ignorant assumption."

I raise my eyebrows, not used to someone so readily admitting any wrongdoing. "It's all good. I'm sure I've made some assumptions about you that aren't true either."

"*Quite* a few, I'm sure." Jasmine laughs. "Can I ask you another question?"

"Shoot."

"What's the deal with Peyton?"

Shit. I didn't think she'd go there. "What do you mean?"

"Like, what's the deal with her dad? Her last name is Devereaux, right? But she calls herself a Callahan and according to Madeline, she and Charles married when Peyton was a baby and he's raised her ever since."

I scoff. A series of nannies have raised Peyton. Neither Madeline nor Charles have any natural instincts when it comes to parenting. I suspect zero interest in the job as well.

"Her dad died when she was a baby—maybe ten or eleven months old, I think."

"Oh." Jazz nibbles her lip and if I weren't driving right now, I'd be tempted to pull it free with my teeth. "So, if her dad is dead, why didn't Charles adopt her and officially make her a Callahan? All three of them put a lot of importance on surnames, especially *that* name."

"It's your name too, you know," I remind her.

"Ugh." She throws her head back into the seat. "Not if I have anything to say about it. Do you know the bastard legally changed my name without asking how I felt about that?"

"It doesn't surprise me in the slightest. In case you haven't noticed, Charles Callahan is rather full of himself."

"You can say that again," she mutters. "Do you know why he never adopted her?"

"I do, actually." I glance at her out of the corner of my eye. "You ever hear of Devereaux Broadcasting?"

She shakes her head.

"It's a giant European media conglomerate," I explain. "The largest, in fact. Peyton's birth father, Pierre Devereaux, owned it, and if she meets the stipulations of his will, she will become the sole heiress of the entire thing. It's worth over twenty billion."

"Whoa. Do you know what she has to do to get it?"

I nod. "It's very specific. First and foremost, she has to retain the Devereaux name since she's the last of the bloodline. Even if she marries."

"That's weird."

I shrug. "It's how it is in our world. Like you said, surnames are *very* important."

"So, that's it? She just keeps her name and she gets billions? He didn't leave anything to Madeline? Weren't they married?"

"They were, but she didn't get a dime because they were married for less than five years." I shake my head, wondering why the hell I'm volunteering all this information. I don't normally offer intel to anyone outside a need to know basis. "Between you and me, that's why Madeline sank her claws into your father. The woman is the textbook definition of a gold digger and unfortunately for her, Pierre's will had that five-year clause. Charles and Madeline were married less than six months after Pierre passed. I'm pretty sure they were having an affair *before* he died, considering he lived in France while she and Peyton were in California.

"As for Peyton, she needs to marry before her nineteenth birthday, and the marriage needs to be legitimate. Then, she needs to produce an heir by twenty-one and ensure that child—and any future heirs—bears the Devereaux name as well."

"Why so young? Was he aware we're living in the twenty-first century?"

"No idea. He was pretty eccentric from what I can tell." I shift my car into park in front of her house. "He was also seventy-two years old when Peyton was born. The guy had a well-documented history of being a stereotypical playboy. I guess he was feeling his mortality and finally decided he'd get married and produce an heir with his pretty young wife before he kicked the bucket."

A crinkle forms between her brows. "Why do *you* know all of this?"

Here's where I decide whether or not to trust her. The only people who know about this are Charles, Madeline, Peyton, me, and the guys. And Reed and Bentley aren't supposed to know, nor do the others know they know. In order for Peyton's marriage to appear legitimate, she needs to keep her mouth tightly closed about our agreement and the reason behind it. But if I do give Jasmine this piece of information, I'll make great strides in earning her trust, which I need.

I clear my throat. "If I tell you this, you cannot say a word. It's serious shit."

"Serious like whatever's going on between our fathers?" I nod. "I promise to keep my mouth shut. You can trust me, Kingston."

I blow out a big breath. "Because Peyton and I made a deal. I agreed to marry her and do whatever was necessary for her to collect her inheritance." When Jazz's jaw drops, I add, "But that deal's off. I have no desire nor intention of *ever* being a part of her life again. I haven't even fucked her in over six months."

"Why? And what were you set to gain from this deal you made, because I *know* you didn't agree to it out of the goodness of your heart."

Fuck, she's too perceptive for her own good. "That's another one of those, *I'll tell you when the time is right* things."

She sighs heavily. "I'm holding you to that, Davenport."

I nod toward the front door. "You should get inside."

Jasmine unfastens her seat belt and shifts toward me. "I know I said it earlier, but thank you again for today. I mean it, Kingston. I don't know how you pulled it off, but that was everything my soul desperately needed and I couldn't be more grateful."

Jazz licks her lips while staring at mine. It'd be so easy to lean over the console and close the gap between us. I bite my tongue, resisting the urge.

I nod toward the front door again. "I'll see you in the morning, okay? Pick you up at the same time?"

She jumps out of the car and nods. "See you then. Goodnight."

I watch her in my rearview as I drive away. Jazz

doesn't make a move to go inside the house until I'm practically out of sight. It's almost as if she's reluctant to see me leave, which is exactly the reaction I was hoping for. Now I need to convince myself that I don't feel the same way. I don't know why the fuck this girl gets to me as much as she does, but I'm starting to hate it less and less, and *that* is crossing into very dangerous territory.

"Fuck." I press the voice command button on my phone. When it beeps, I say, "Call John P."

"Calling John P.," Siri replies.

"Davenport," my PI says in greeting. "I've been waiting for your call."

"Did you get any hits?"

John barks out a laugh. "Yeah, I got some hits. A lot of them, in fact."

"Tell me about it."

He clears his throat. "Well, first of all, I did confirm Mahalia Rivera was employed as a maid in the Callahan mansion. Everything seems legit on that end, but she was young—just turned eighteen when she started. The girl was born about six months later."

"Where was she before that?"

"Foster system," he says. "Abandoned as an infant. Bounced around a lot—never in the same home for more than a couple months. Was listed as a runaway for about four months before she aged out."

I stretch my neck from side to side. Well, that confirms my suspicions on how Jasmine's mother came into Charles Callahan's life. She would've been the perfect target—young, beautiful, no one to care about her whereabouts. I have no doubt she *ran away* to be with a man over twice her age who made a lot of promises he had no intention of keeping.

"What else?"

He clears his throat. "According to her tax records, she listed that same Hidden Hills address on her returns for three years straight. The next year, and every year thereafter, she used an address in south Los Angeles."

What the fuck?

"She lived there for *three years*?"

I wasn't expecting that. That would mean Jasmine lived in that mansion during the first few years of her life. Peyton and Madeline would've also been there at that point. Madeline had to have known Jazz was Charles's kid. There's no way that woman would've permitted a maid to live there with a kid in tow. Knowing that, she's also aware of her husband's proclivity toward fucking teenagers. It makes me wonder what other information she's privy to.

"Yep," John confirms. "Slightly over. And here's the kicker: an affidavit of paternity was filed shortly before Rivera's death. Callahan had his name added to the girl's birth certificate."

Why the hell would he do that? Now I'm really fucking confused.

I pull into my garage and shift into park. "Do you know the cause of death?"

"Gunshot wound. Police are calling it a stray bullet from a drive-by. She was shot in the head while waiting at a bus stop one morning. Pronounced dead at the scene."

I scrub a hand over my face. "Fuck."

This conversation is triggering something in the back of my head, but I can't put my finger on it.

My head jerks up when it hits me. "John, I gotta go. I want a tail on Madeline Callahan."

"Am I supposed to be looking for anything in particular?"

I shake my head. "I don't know yet. I just want to know what she's up to. Who she's spending time with. Get back to me if you find something suspicious."

"Will do."

I end the call and rush through the property until I get to the pool house. I head into my closet and pull down some boxes from the top shelf. My dad's second wife, bitch that she was, wanted no trace of Jennifer Davenport in the house. My dad would've been fine tossing everything into the garbage. Thankfully, my sister turned on the waterworks and begged him to let us sort through everything. Tough task for a pair of nine-year-olds, but that's my dickheaded father for you.

We donated most of our mom's belongings but Ainsley kept all of the jewelry and the photo albums went into these boxes, which I've kept in my closet. Every once in a while, I'll go through them, usually around the anniversary of her death when I'm feeling her loss even harder. I sit on the floor, flipping through one album after another until I get to the right age range. After a good thirty minutes, I finally find the picture I was thinking of.

My mom is standing next to another woman who I now know is Mahalia Rivera. Jazz has a framed picture with her mom and sister on the desk in her bedroom. I had this weird déjà vu moment when I first saw it as I was snooping around, but I assumed it was simply because Jazz resembles her mother so much. In the photo I have, there are also three children. Me, Ainsley, and a little girl who has to be Jasmine. I once asked my dad who the other woman was and he simply said, "A friend of your mother's."

Holy fuck.

My sister and I used to play with Jazz. Is that why I feel so drawn to her? Because somehow, even though we were so young, my subconscious somehow remembers her? Right when I thought I had this situation with my father and Charles Callahan figured out, another wrench gets thrown into the mix.

Could this shit get any more convoluted?

chapter twenty

JAZZ

I can't stop thinking about my outing with Belle and Kingston yesterday. I smile fondly as I pick up the picture on my desk. Belle, our mom, and I are high above the ocean sitting in one of the cabs of the Pacific Park Ferris wheel. Every year on my birthday, we would spend the day on the Santa Monica Pier. It was our thing for as long as I can remember. We didn't have much—hardly anything, really—but she'd work over-time just to get enough cash for a few unlimited ride bracelets followed by churros and ice cream.

God, I miss her.

What is Kingston up to? You can't threaten some-body one minute then do the nicest thing possible for them the next. And what about all that information he divulged regarding his arrangement with Peyton? I know he's trying to keep me from snooping around

207

whatever our fathers are up to, but this seems a bit extreme. I know he has some sort of motive—I'll just have to keep my guard up until I figure out what that is.

There's a knock on my bedroom door right before Ms. Williams says, "Miss Jasmine, your presence is required in the dining room in exactly ten minutes."

What the hell? I usually don't eat breakfast before school—maybe a quick apple if anything. Ms. Williams knows that. Plus, since I've been here, I haven't seen anyone eating breakfast in the dining room on a school day.

I open my door. "Why?"

Ms. Williams frowns. "It's not my place to question Mr. Callahan. All I know is that he has requested both yours and Peyton's presence at breakfast this morning."

"Requested, as in, it's optional?" I raise an eyebrow in challenge.

Her eyes narrow. "No, young lady, it's *not* optional." She looks at the slim watch on her wrist. "You now have nine minutes, so I suggest you finish getting ready for school."

I sigh. "Fine. I'll be there."

Ms. Williams nods and turns on her heel. I was ready before she knocked, so after quickly checking my reflection and grabbing my backpack, I head downstairs. Kingston will be here to pick me up soon so thankfully, I won't have to suffer through sitting with those people for long. We haven't shared a meal together since the night Kingston and his dad were here. It doesn't seem to be a big thing in this household unless we have guests, which is perfectly fine with me.

Charles is reading something on his iPad when I arrive. He looks up when I enter the room and sets the device on the table.

"Jasmine."

"Morning," I mumble as I take a seat at the opposite end of the table.

A chill races down my spine when we make eye contact. He's looking at me like he's trying to read my mind. Does he know Kingston and I were spying on him the other night?

Madeline and Peyton walk into the room, breaking our stare-off, and take their seats as well. Madeline sits next to my father and Peyton sits directly across from me, no doubt so she has a direct line of sight to glare at me.

"Good morning, everyone." Madeline flashes a fake smile and turns to her husband. "Dear, what's the meaning of this? The girls have to leave soon."

"Are you questioning me, *dear*?" Charles gives his wife a look that erases the smile on her face.

"No, of course not," she sputters, redirecting her gaze to the white tablecloth.

His blue eyes narrow. "I should hope not, considering it's not your place."

"Of course not, dear. I apologize for my indiscretion." Madeline is still in a subservient position, carefully avoiding his eyes.

Whoa, what's that about?

"Good morning, Daddy," Peyton says enthusiastically. "Thank you for inviting us to eat with you this morning. Seeing you always brightens my day."

Kiss ass.

Charles smiles at her. "Good morning, Peyton. I'm glad to see at least one of the women in this household has some manners."

Peyton beams while I frown. What is going on right now? It's not like these people are exactly warm by nature, but there seems to be a considerable amount of tension between him and Madeline.

Natalie, the chef's assistant, rolls a cart into the room and sets a dish in front of each one of us. Charles's plate is filled with a giant omelet, hash browns, bacon, and fruit. Damn, that looks good. The rest of us have a scoop of cottage cheese with a few berries on top.

"Eat up, girls. As my wife so *helpfully* reminded me, we don't have much time." He waits until we each take a bite. "Now, as for the reason I called you here, I wanted to check in with you. I've been out of town so much recently, I feel out of the loop. Jasmine, you've been here for a couple of weeks now, how are you settling in?"

"Um... fine."

Charles raises an eyebrow. "And school? How's that

going?"

"Yeah, Jasmine, how's school going?" Peyton goads.

I bounce her fake smile right back at her. "It's just great, thank you for asking."

"I'm glad to hear that," Charles says.

Madeline lifts her eyes to her daughter. "How is Kingston, dear? Have you two discussed what color theme you're going with for homecoming?"

Peyton huffs and jerks her head in my direction. "You should ask the boyfriend thief over there."

Madeline turns to me, confusion evident in her expression. "What does that mean?"

I shrug. "I have no idea. Kingston dumped her, so it seems like she's looking for someone to blame."

Peyton's face turns red. "He did *not* dump me! We mutually decided to take a break."

I scoff. Sheesh, this girl is delusional. "Sure, let's go with that."

Madeline looks back at Peyton. "You two broke up again? I thought you had settled your... issues."

Peyton moves the berries around on her plate. "Just temporarily. I've given him permission to sow his oats, or whatever, before we graduate and it's time to get serious." She looks me directly in the eye. "You might have his attention now, but that won't last. You can't keep him. He *always* comes back to me."

"I don't *want* him. How many times do I have to tell you that?"

She rolls her eyes. "Right. Then why are you hanging out with him?"

I grind my teeth. "We're... friends. I'm also friends with his sister. Are you going to accuse me of wanting Ainsley as well?"

Madeline clears her throat. "Jasmine, I didn't realize you and Kingston were spending time together. When did that start?"

"This week." I shrug. "It's no big deal. We hung out *once*. And my seven-year-old sister was with us almost the entire time."

Peyton's jaw drops. "Kingston doesn't like little kids. Why would he spend time with one?"

I smirk. "Hmm, that's weird, because if you ask me, he's pretty great with 'em."

Madeline looks upset, but for some reason, Charles looks pleased with this bit of information.

Charles takes a sip of his coffee. "Well, I'm glad to hear you're making friends, Jasmine. Kingston Davenport is a fine young man. I approve of your association with him."

I give him a look that says, *Gee, thanks, because your approval makes my life complete.*

"Daddy!" Peyton shouts.

Charles rolls his eyes. "Oh, don't be such a poor sport, Peyton. Men aren't built to be monogamous. If Kingston wants to spend a little time with Jasmine—or any other girl, for that matter—it's none of your business. Trying to force his hand will accomplish nothing. You know better than to expect otherwise."

I bite my tongue to prevent myself from going off on his misogynistic ass.

Peyton's nostrils flare before she schools her expression and smiles. "You're right, Daddy. Of course."

He nods. "Of course I'm right."

Ms. Williams walks into the room. "Excuse the interruption, but the younger Mr. Davenport just pulled into the driveway."

Thank God.

My fork clinks on my plate when I drop it. "That's my ride."

Madeline and Peyton gasp in unison.

Sperm Donor smiles. "You may be excused, Jasmine. Have a great day at school."

I grab my bag from beneath the table and pull it over my shoulder. "Yeah... thanks."

I can't escape the Twilight Zone fast enough. I step out the front door right as Kingston is pulling up.

God, I wish I didn't find his car so sexy, but I do. *I really do.* I fumble for a minute before I can figure out how to open the door before sliding into the passenger seat.

"Hey." Kingston's eyes are glued to my thighs.

I yank my plaid skirt back into place. It had ridden up as I was getting into the car. I need to be more cautious—I'm still not used to wearing these damn things every day.

"Hey. You showed up just in time to save me from the most awkward breakfast ever. I'm pretty sure Peyton was ready to claw my eyes out."

Kingston shifts into gear. "Since when do the Callahans have weekday breakfast together?"

"Since today, apparently." I shrug. "My sperm donor wanted to 'check in' with us."

He frowns. "Check in on *what*, exactly?"

"He asked me how school was going, how I'm settling in. Stuff like that. Then, you got brought up and the tension quadrupled. Fun times." I make a funny face. "Not."

Kingston raises his brows. "How did I get brought up?"

"I don't remember exactly... Madeline asked Peyton something about homecoming. Then Peyton accused me of trying to steal you away from her, which led to Charles spouting off some sexist bullshit about men being incapable of monogamy."

He belts out a laugh.

I narrow my eyes at him. "Don't tell me you agree with that prick."

Kingston's lips turn up in a grin. "I definitely don't agree with him. That's a blanket statement for pretty much everything. Speaking of homecoming... you get a dress yet?"

"Why would I do that?"

He looks at me as if I'm dense. "Because that's what girls do."

"Yeah, well, I'm not most girls."

"I've noticed," he says matter-of-factly. "But you need to get one anyway."

I cross my arms over my chest. "Why is that? I have no intention of going."

"Why the hell not?"

"Why the hell should I?" I challenge.

"Jesus Christ, woman." Kingston blows out a breath. "You need to get a dress because I need a date and I want *you* to be that date."

I shake my head. "I'm sorry... I thought I left Bizzarro World back at the house. What in the hell are you talking about?"

Kingston scrubs a hand down his face in frustration. "Are you going to fight me at every turn? Why are you being so damn difficult?"

"Uh... because you can't always get what you want? Why would you want *me* to be your date anyway? You don't even like me."

He gives me a wry look. "We both know that's not true."

I shake my head. "Fine. Your dick likes me. But the rest of you thinks I'm *trash*, remember?"

"Fucking aggravating, stubborn ass woman," he mutters.

"Well, if I'm so fucking aggravating, why are we even talking?"

"Fine. I'll shut up then."

I look out the window. "Great. Then it's agreed: no talking."

Kingston cranks the stereo and we finish the drive to school without saying another word. When we pull into a parking spot, I go to open my door but he manacles my wrists, preventing me from moving.

"What are you doing, jackass? Let go!"

"Just fucking hold on a second!" He tightens his grip when I put more effort into my struggle. "Look, I'm sorry, okay? Happy?"

I stop squirming. "Sorry for *what?*"

"For assuming you'd want to go to homecoming with me. For trying to strong-arm you into going." He heaves out a breath. "I'm not used to working so hard to get a girl's attention, all right? You've gotta give me some room to fuck up."

"I don't need to give you room for *anything*, Kingston. I never asked for your attention. I don't *want* your attention."

His jaw clenches. "Don't lie to yourself, Jazz. We both know your body wants my attention *very* much. In fact, I'd bet you thought about me all night after I dropped you off. That when you stuck your fingers inside your wet little pussy, you wished they were mine."

My mouth gapes. Mostly because he's right, but I'm not about to admit that.

"You're an egotistical asshole."

Kingston gives me a wicked grin. "But I'm *right*. Admit it."

I look away. "I'm not admitting shit."

He adjusts his grip until both of my wrists are now clenched in one of his hands. With the other hand, he puts pressure on my chin until I turn back to him.

His hazel eyes twinkle. "Admit it."

"*No.*"

Kingston laughs. "Fine, then I'll prove my point another way."

In the next moment, he unfastens his seat belt and leans over the console to slam his lips against mine. I'm so shocked, it takes me a second to figure out what's happening. Once I do, I tell myself to pull away—or punch him in the nuts—but instead, I'm moaning into his mouth, deepening the kiss. When he releases my wrists, I undo my seat belt and take fistfuls of his hair, pulling myself closer.

He groans when I tug harder as his lips travel down the slope of my neck. "Jasmine..." Kiss. "Will you please..." Kiss. "Go to homecoming with me?" Kiss.

"*No.*" I gasp when he bites down, before licking the sting away.

"Are you saying you need more convincing? Because I'm definitely up for that." Kingston pulls back and nods to his growing erection, clearly outlined in his black chinos.

"I am *not* having sex with you, so you'll need to take care of your little problem some other way."

He grins. "Jazz, as you may recall, there's nothing *little* about me. Shit, at Donovan's party, you couldn't stop telling me how much you loved my *huge* dick."

I flush in anger. Or maybe arousal. Nope, let's go with anger. I narrow my eyes at him, irritated at the reminder of the night I *still* can't remember. I can't believe I didn't think to grill him about it before now.

"What *really* happened that night? Don't bullshit me."

He flips down his visor and fixes the mess I made of his hair. "You saw the pictures. *And video.* I think it's pretty obvious what happened."

"C'mon, Kingston. You say I need to trust you. Well, you need to *earn* that trust. Tell me the truth. I *know* I didn't have sex with either one of you. Why can't you just admit that?"

He searches my eyes for a moment. "You're not ready for the truth."

Ugh. Infuriating man!

"I'm a lot stronger than you seem to think." I flip my visor and smooth out my hair. "And until you're ready to provide some answers, I have nothing to say to you."

I exit the vehicle and cringe when I see a large crowd gathered around Kingston's car. Peyton and her squad are up front, trying to murder me with their eyes. I stifle a groan when I realize all these people just saw me and Kingston making out. Crap, why do I lose all sense when he touches me?

Kingston gets out of the car and barks, "Back the fuck up."

I'm still frozen in place as he grabs my hand. The crowd parts like the Red Sea as he pulls me behind him, not releasing me until we're standing in front of my locker.

He nods toward my locker. "Hurry up and get whatever shit you need. I'll walk you to class."

"I don't need you to walk me *anywhere*. Don't you think you've caused enough trouble this morning? It's bad enough that you think you can kiss me without my consent, but it's even worse you did it in front of half the school!"

"Why do you give a shit what they think?"

"I *don't* give a shit what they think," I whisper-shout. "But I also don't want to give them any more fodder. I'm sick of the bullshit. I don't need any extra drama in my life. I never asked for any of it. All I want is to go to class, get good grades, and be invisible."

Kingston stares at me for a moment. "Jazz, one thing you could *never* be is invisible."

I scoff. "I don't see why—"

"Yo, Jazzy Jazz," Bentley interrupts, swinging his arm over my shoulders. "What's all the fuss about this morning? I heard you were playing tonsil hockey in the parking lot with this asshole." He jerks his chin toward Kingston, who's pinning him with a glare. "I was trying to get some morning head behind the gym but all the boujee bitches in the house were too busy gossiping. You two lovebirds are ruining my game."

"Fuck off, Fitzgerald," Kingston snaps.

Bentley laughs. "Calm down there, big guy. I'm just stating the facts." He leans down to whisper in my ear. "You know, if you're looking for someone to make out with, I'd be happy to volunteer as tribute. You don't need to put up with this broody bastard if you want some lovin'."

I push him away with a smile, despite my best intentions to keep a straight face. "Shut up, you idiot."

Bentley gasps dramatically. "Ouch, new girl. That hurts." When the warning bell rings, he places a quick kiss on my cheek. "Gotta go, babe. See you at lunch."

Bentley laughs when Kingston flips him off.

"Get your shit and let's go," he growls.

I narrow my eyes. "Stop bossing me around."

"Stop being so fucking stubborn."

I punch in the code to open my locker, grab composition notebooks for my first two classes and a calculator. I shove them in my bag and slam the door shut.

Kingston is glued to my side as I walk to statistics, but I'm so irritated with him, I say nothing. I know pretty much every set of eyes are on us, but I ignore them as well. I'm almost relieved when we get to my class and Kingston takes off, until I step into the room and see that people are no less curious than they were in the hallway. I'm sure they're all just as dumbfounded as I am, wondering why Kingston went from bullying me one day, to making out with me in the parking lot. Then, you have Bentley, who won't stop openly flirting with me and pressing his lips to my cheek every chance he gets.

What was I thinking accepting a ride from Kingston this morning? I should've known better after what happened yesterday, but I was riding on such a high from seeing my sister when he mentioned it, I agreed without any regard for consequence. I need to put a stop to this. I need to distance myself from Kingston, no matter how pushy he is or how attracted I am to him. I pull out my phone when I get to my desk and surreptitiously text Ainsley, asking for a ride home. I sigh in relief when she immediately agrees.

With that settled, I open my Chromebook and notebook, ready to begin class.

chapter twenty-one

JAZZ

On my way to lunch, I stop in the ladies' room to relieve my aching bladder. After doing my business and washing my hands, I'm just about to head into the dining hall when three snobby bitches saunter in, claws ready to lash out. No, make that... five... seven... ten. As the last one enters, she locks the door behind her. I recognize a few of them from classes we share, but not some of the younger looking ones.

Shit.

No matter how scrappy I can be, ten-to-one odds aren't good for anyone.

I paste false bravado on my face as I address Peyton, the obvious ringleader of this little confrontation.

"What do you want, Peyton?"

"Hmm, now isn't that a loaded question?" she

muses, tapping her chin in thought. "Well, for starters, I'd like you to drop dead just like your mommy."

Her words rob me of breath. It doesn't surprise me that she would use my mother to hurt me, but it definitely has the intended effect. I can't let that distract me though—I need to get the hell out of this bathroom.

I sigh in mock boredom. "Look, Peyton. I'm not really in the mood to deal with you and your merry band of bitches. Why don't you just say what you came in here to say and we can all be on our way?"

She smiles coldly. "Now, where's the fun in that?"

My phone buzzes from the pocket inside my blazer. I'm sure it's Ainsley wondering where the hell I am, but I'm not going to risk taking my attention away from Peyton to check.

"I don't have time for this." I roll my eyes and start walking forward, deciding to just push through them.

"Not so fast, slut," Peyton sneers. "Too bad your precious kings aren't here to protect you now, isn't it?"

Each girl moves in freakish harmony to form a human wall. On the inside, my nerves are frayed but I do my best to project a cool surface.

I scoff. "I don't need them to protect me."

"I think you'll be singing a different tune by the time we're done with you. Unless..."

"Unless *what*?"

My phone is vibrating like crazy now.

"Unless you stay away from Kingston," she replies.

"We'll let you walk out of here if you promise you won't go near him ever again."

"And Bentley," Whitney adds.

"And Bentley," Peyton echoes.

I meet her hate-filled gaze dead on. "What are you going to do if I don't? Beat me up? Break my nose, maybe? An eye for an eye? Is that it?"

I know I'm about to get my ass kicked, but I'm sure as fuck not going down without a fight. I curl my hand into a fist, positioning my thumb over the first two fingers.

A genuine grin stretches across her face. This psycho is actually enjoying this. "It's a good place to start."

The bathroom door starts jiggling, someone's fists pounding on the other side. "Jazz, are you in there?"

Oh, thank fuck. Ainsley can get a janitor to unlock the door. Hopefully I can hold these chicks off until then.

"I'm locked in—" I start to scream.

"Jazz?" Ainsley repeats, panic evident in her voice. "Are you okay?"

Peyton lunges for me, knowing her window is closing, but I dodge her punch.

"Grab her arms, you idiots!" she screams.

It takes four girls to properly restrain me but when they finally do, Peyton bitch slaps me across the face before she punches me right in the stomach, forcing me to double over. Damn it, that hurt. She must have been watching YouTube videos on how to properly throw a punch.

As I'm gasping for breath, the door slams open, several girls grunting as they're jostled forward violently. Unfortunately for me, their forward momentum causes my head to slam into the wall.

I groan as spots flicker before my eyes. "Jesus."

I glance toward the doorway and see Kingston, Bentley, and Reed, each staring at the girls with pure fury in their gaze.

"Get out," Kingston says without any inflection whatsoever. I don't know why, but his quiet tone makes him seem even more dangerous.

The crowd scurries as all three guys step into the bathroom. Before Peyton can get away, Kingston steps in her path.

"I'll deal with you later," he promises.

Peyton blanches. "Baby, it's not what it looks like. I—"

Kingston's fists clench as he takes a step toward her. "Save it, Peyton. Get the fuck out of my face before I do something that can't be undone."

Her eyes widen before she too, runs out the door.

I flinch when Kingston approaches me and gently runs a finger over my cheek. He frowns as he inspects what I'm sure is a Peyton-sized handprint.

"You okay?" he asks.

My head aches and I feel bruised where Peyton hit me, but other than that, I'm okay.

"Yeah." I sigh when he places a soft kiss right between my eyebrows. "How'd you get the door unlocked?"

Bentley shakes a key ring. "Master keys. I've had these babies since freshman year. They come in handy when you want to fool around in an empty classroom or closet."

I have no words for this sex-crazed fool.

"Oh my God, Jazz, are you okay?" Ainsley runs into the room, pushing her brother aside. "What the hell happened?"

"They cornered me," I say. "How'd you know where to find me?"

Ainsley and Kingston share a look before he says, "I installed a tracker on your phone."

My jaw drops. "You what?!"

He raises an eyebrow. "It proved to be useful, didn't it?"

I narrow my eyes. "But that doesn't explain *why* you did it."

"Baby girl, let's not worry about Kingston's stalker tendencies right now." Bentley pulls me into a side hug. "We all know you're not going to get an answer until he's ready to give you an answer. What do you say we ditch the last few classes? We'll grab an ice pack for that beautiful cheek of yours and I'll buy you a big, greasy burger at In-N-Out." As if on cue, my stomach growls, making him laugh. "See, your stomach likes this idea."

"Fine," I mutter. "But only because I'm hungry."

"I wanna come," Ainsley says. "Jazz, you can ride with me."

Bentley glances at Ainsley. "I think Jazz should ride with me. You can take Reed."

Rich kid problems: driving fancy sports cars that only have two seats.

"Okay." Ainsley looks at Kingston. "You coming, bro?"

Kingston's eyes haven't left me yet. "No. I have something to take care of. I'll catch up with you guys later." He steps into me again and presses his forehead to mine. It's a surprisingly intimate gesture—one I have no idea how to respond to. "Give us a minute."

Nobody dares to question him. They simply leave the bathroom without a word.

"What are you—"

He presses his index finger to my lips. "Are you really okay? You looked pretty shaken up when I first arrived."

"Yeah… well..." I shrug. "Being trapped in a small room with ten crazy bitches isn't exactly the most comforting feeling."

He runs his fingers over my cheek again. "Are you hurt anywhere else?"

"I hit the back of my head on the wall, but it's fine. Peyton landed a pretty solid punch to my stomach, but that's all she could do before you came barging in."

Kingston crouches down and untucks my shirt.

I bat his hands away. "What are you doing?"

He gives me his *I'm in charge* look that I'm beginning to know so well. "Let me see."

I sigh, knowing that arguing with him on this is stupid. I lift my shirt, holding it up right beneath my breasts. Kingston's jaw clenches as he sees the red bruise blooming on my right side. I wince when he presses down slightly.

"Does it hurt much?"

I shake my head. "I'll be fine."

Kingston stares at my stomach for a moment before pressing a kiss to the injured area. I gasp when his lips linger, sliding back and forth.

"Kingston, what are you doing?"

I can feel his smile against my skin. "Kissing it better."

My lips curl upward. "Well, as nice as the thought is, I don't need you to kiss my boo boos. I'm a big girl—I can take care of myself."

"What if I *want* to take care of you?" he murmurs, tugging the waistband of my skirt down so he can press his lips to my hipbone. "What if I want you to be mine?"

"*What?*"

I suppress a moan when he starts bunching my skirt and peppering my thigh with kisses. I need to get away from him before I do something stupid—like, I don't know, letting him eat me out on the bathroom floor—so I sidestep him, breaking the contact.

"Quit screwing around. Ainsley and the guys are probably standing right outside the door waiting. Didn't you say you had something you needed to take care of?"

He stands up and not so discreetly adjusts himself. "I do. Go eat."

"You sure you don't want to come?" When he smirks, I add, "To *lunch?*"

He nods. "I'm sure. If Peyton gives you any more trouble at home, I need you to tell me immediately. I don't like that you're vulnerable in that house. Make sure you keep your bedroom door locked."

I fold my arms over my chest. "I don't need a knight in shining armor to fight my battles for me."

Kingston gives me a wicked grin. "I never claimed to be a knight. I'd rather be someone's *nightmare* and Peyton is high on my shit list right now."

"Why? Why do you care what she does to me?"

He wraps his hand around the doorknob. "Because whether you want to admit it or not, Jasmine, you're *mine*, which means you're under my protection. Peyton and every other person in this school knows that, but she got cocky, formed an army, and deemed you a target. Doing so is a direct slap in the face to me, and I will *not* be disrespected. She and her little followers need a reminder of who's really running the show around here."

"What are you going to do?"

"If I tell you... I'd have to kill you. And I rather like

230

keeping you around." He winks before walking out of the room.

Did Mr. Serious actually crack a joke?

What in the ever-loving fuck is happening with this guy, and why am I thrilled by the possibilities?

Good Lord, I'm in trouble.

~

"She actually said that?" Ainsley pops a fry into her mouth.

I finish chewing before replying. "Yep."

Ainsley frowns. "What a bitch. I'm so glad my brother finally stopped worrying about what other people think and dumped her ass."

I just finished recapping the whole bathroom incident while eating lunch with Ainsley, Reed, and Bentley. The guys share a look as if they're biting back their own comments. Do they know about the deal Kingston made with Peyton?

"Peyton's behavior doesn't surprise me in the least," Reed says. "But Whitney striking out on her own does."

I also told them about Whitney rallying our classmates to taunt me.

"Maybe she'll realize the error of her ways the next time she gets thirsty and I won't let her milk me dry." Bentley takes a giant bite of his Animal Style burger.

Reed laughs. "Yeah, right. I've *never* seen you turn down pussy."

"It's true!" he insists through a mouthful of food. "I wouldn't do that to Jazzy Jazz. Besides, it's not like I don't have back up."

I roll my eyes. "You're a pig."

"So you've told me." Bentley gets a devious smile on his face. "You know what I think?"

I raise my eyebrows. "No, but I'm sure you'll tell me."

He chuckles. "I think you need to teach them a lesson. You and Kingston should lay it on really thick. Make them think you're both fucking *and* catching feelings. Once people see that you have Kingston wrapped around your finger, Peyton's followers will jump ship. They'll want to worship the girl who got the king's attention."

I scoff. "Uh, no thanks. I have no desire to play mind games, nor do I need anyone to worship me."

"Why not?" Bentley asks. "Sometimes you have to fight dirty. Especially with those catty bitches."

Ainsley points a fry at Bentley. "I'm gonna agree with him there. Sometimes you have to stoop to their level."

I shake my head. "Still not interested. Besides, the thought of *anyone* having Kingston wrapped around their finger is laughable."

Bentley smirks. "I wouldn't be so sure about that, boo." He picks his phone up from the table when it vibrates. "Speaking of..." Bentley runs his thumbs over the screen for a moment before standing up and shoving it in his pocket. "I gotta head out—we're being summoned. C'mon, Reed."

Reed takes one more bite of his burger before shoving it back in the bag. "I'll see you later, Ains?"

Ainsley smiles shyly. "Uh, yeah, sure."

He nods to me. "Bye, Jazz."

I wait until the guys are out of earshot before I lay into her. "What was *that* about?"

She blushes. "He's been watching me rehearse. It's no big deal."

My eyes widen. "How long has that been going on?"

"The last two weeks or so. He's only shown up a few times."

"What does your brother think of you getting it on with his bestie?"

"I'm not banging Reed!" she insists.

I lean back in my chair and smile. "But you *want* to. What about Donovan?"

She frowns. "I haven't heard from Donovan since I returned the keys to his pool house."

"What? I thought he was really into you?"

"I think he was more into the thrill of the chase."

I give her a sad smile. "I'm sorry. It's his loss."

"It's all good. I had to lose my virginity to someone. At least I got a couple of orgasms out of it."

My eyes widen. "What?! You were a virgin before that? Why didn't you say something?"

"Because I didn't want to make a big deal out of it and chicken out. I've been wanting to give it up for a while now, but the guy I was interested in wasn't biting. So... I gave it to someone who did."

"You wanted it to be Reed, didn't you?"

She sighs. "Yeah, and I know he likes me, but he has this weird thing about not disrespecting my brother, which is totally lame. It's none of Kingston's business who I date. Plus, Reed was fucking around with Imogen. Who knows... he still might be."

"But he watches your ballet rehearsals? Why would he do that if he didn't want to pursue something with you?"

Ainsley shrugs. "Ironically, spending the night with Donovan seems to have triggered something. Reed *never* initiated contact with me before—that was always on me and he'd always tell me nothing could happen between us. Since that party, he's been...different. Texts me a lot, shows up at my rehearsal. He even asked if I wanted to grab dinner tonight afterward. We've never eaten a meal together without someone else present, usually Kingston and Bentley."

I shake my head. "In other words, he saw that you were moving on and decided he'd better act quickly before he loses his shot."

"Maybe. Reed's a hard guy to decode. He's always so damn stoic."

"He's definitely that." I laugh. "So he no longer cares about your brother's opinion?"

"I plan on finding out tonight at dinner, one way or the other. He may not want to see me with other guys, but I'm not going to wait around for someone who will never claim me. If Reed can't grow a pair and tell my brother to fuck off with his, 'My sister is off-limits,' bullshit, then fuck him. I'm not going to pine for him while he's out screwing Imogen or whoever else. It's not fair." She releases a heavy sigh. "Enough about my boy problems. What's going on with you and my brother? And don't you dare try telling me *nothing* again. I've never seen him act like he does around you. I still can't believe he took you to see your sister."

I groan. "I don't know, Ains. I think he's a jerk more often than not and I don't trust him, but then he does something so unexpectantly sweet like taking me to see Belle, not to mention how great he was with her. And today—he looked like he was going to murder Peyton on the spot when he burst into that bathroom. When he got to me, when he hovered over me protectively, with a gentleness I would've never thought he was capable of, it confused me. *He* confuses me."

Ainsley scrunches her face. "Boys are stupid."

I clink my soda cup against hers. "I'll drink to that."

chapter twenty-two

KINGSTON

"What's the plan?" Reed takes a drag from his joint.

We're standing in the Windsor parking lot, right outside of the gym, waiting for Peyton to get out of cheerleading practice.

I look at him out of the corner of my eye. "I'm just going to have a few words with her."

"Why'd you need us for that?"

"Because we need to present a united front. These people need to know that if anyone fucks with Jazz, they're going to have to deal with all three of us."

"Man, I've never wanted to hit a girl before, but *that* girl tempts me," Bentley adds. "I can't believe she ganged up on Jasmine like that. I mean, I'm all for chick fights because they're totally hot, but locking her in a room and expecting her to fight off ten bitches at once is just bullshit. Even I'm not that fucking shady."

I raise an eyebrow. "You two know you need to cut off Whitney and Imogen as well, right? They're just as guilty."

"Already did," Reed says.

"On the same page, brother," Bentley adds.

Speaking of shady bitches... a group of cheerleaders just walked out of the gym. Peyton freezes when she spots us, causing the others to slam into her back. I can tell she's scared but she's so concerned about appearances, she pastes a fake ass smile on her face and walks over here, swaying her hips dramatically.

"Hey, guys," she says. "What are you doing here?"

"We need to have a word, Peyton."

Whitney joins us and curls her arm around Bentley's. "Hey, baby."

He shoves her off of him. "Get the fuck off me, whore. I don't need whatever STD you're carrying this week."

A collective gasp rings throughout the crowd. Seven of the girls in that bathroom today were cheerleaders, which is exactly why I chose this moment to have this conversation. I wanted them to witness their supposed queens' humiliation.

Whitney's jaw drops. "What the hell, Bentley?"

Bentley's eyes run the length of her body with disinterest. "I'm done slumming it with you, Whit. I can no longer pretend that your loose-as-fuck pussy turns me on. You should probably get that shit checked out

238

by a doctor. I hear vaginal reconstruction surgery is all the rage these days."

Bentley may be easy-going for the most part, but the guy is a mean fuck when he wants to be. Dude's got his own demons just waiting to burst out.

Whitney's face flushes and her eyes fill with tears when the laughter begins. The entire football team has now joined the audience. The fact that Imogen is trying to blend in with the masses does not go unnoticed.

"What do you want, Kingston?" Peyton shouts. "Why are you guys being such assholes?"

I smirk, but there's no mirth behind it. "Oh, Peyton, I think you know *exactly* why we're here."

She folds her arms across her overinflated chest. "You're actually defending that piece of trash?"

"Jasmine has more class than you *ever* will," I seethe. "And I came here today to tell you that if you *ever* fuck with her again, you'll be answering to me." I look over the crowd. "That applies to every-fucking-one of you."

Peyton releases a scream so high-pitched, I'm surprised windows aren't breaking right now. "You can't be fucking serious, Kingston! What the hell kind of voodoo pussy is that bitch rocking?"

Bentley and Reed hop into Bentley's Porsche, instinctively knowing I'm about done here.

I flip the Agera door open and give Peyton one last look of revulsion before saying, "I can have that crown you're so fond of, ripped off of your bleached blonde head at the snap of my fingers. Don't test me, Peyton. You won't like the outcome."

With that, the guys and I peel out of the parking lot without a backward glance.

≈

"I never got a chance to ask you. How'd your date with Jazzy Jazz go the other night?"

Bentley throws his controller to the side when I score another touchdown on Madden. After Peyton's verbal beatdown earlier, he and I came back to his place to hang. Reed claimed to have dinner plans with his mom, but I'm not buying it. He and my sister have been acting really weird lately and I intend to figure out what that shit's about.

I take a long pull from my beer. "It wasn't a date."

He laughs. "Right."

"It wasn't," I repeat. "It's all part of the plan. I need to keep her close to ensure she doesn't go running her mouth and fuck everything up for me."

Bentley rolls his eyes. "C'mon, dawg. Are you really going to play it like that? You're into this girl—why is that so hard for you to admit?"

Because she makes me lose sight of my goal, and I don't like that.

I grunt in response, earning another laugh from this asshole.

"How'd you know about her little sister anyway?"

I pick at the label on the bottle. "John dug it up. Jasmine's call history showed multiple attempts to reach the kid's father, but they only connected once. When I showed up at his house, he admitted she was trying to arrange a visit, but he claimed not to have the time to deal with it. He changed his tune really fast when I pulled out a wad of bills. Miraculously, he agreed to allow Jazz weekly visits with her sister as long as the money keeps coming."

Bentley frowned. "Why would he want to keep them away from each other? You'd think at the very least, he'd like getting a free babysitter out of it."

I shrug. "I get the impression it's a power play... like, he wants leverage over Jazz. The way he looks at her isn't right."

He raises his eyebrows. "Like in a skeevy way?"

I nod. "Exactly. It was almost identical to how my dad looked at her. I wanted to knock his fucking teeth out."

"You wanted to knock his teeth out... for a girl you have *no* feelings for whatsoever?"

"Just because I don't have any feelings for her, doesn't mean I want her to become some sick fuck's plaything." I take another drink of my beer. "Speaking of sick fucks... you won't believe what John dug up on Jasmine's mom."

"Are you waiting for a fucking invitation? Spill."

"Get this—for whatever reason, Callahan didn't follow his typical pattern with Jasmine's mom—besides the fact that she was only seventeen, maybe eighteen when he brought her in. She lived with him for over three *years* in the mansion. *And* she was formally employed as a live-in maid until shortly after Jazz's second birthday, which means Jazz also lived at that house. Even *after* Charles married Madeline. I found a picture of me and Ains playing with Jasmine as a toddler. I'm pretty sure Jazz has no fucking clue. As far as she's concerned, they first met after her mom died."

"Oh snap," Bentley mutters. "This shit is complicated."

"No kidding," I agree. "My PI dug up some other stuff that makes it even worse. My head's been spinning nonstop."

"Jazzy Jazz's arrival sure shakes things up, doesn't it?"

"That's an understatement."

"Speaking of shaking this up... you takin' her to Reed's party on Friday?"

Reed's parents are going away for the weekend. He's the only one of us who doesn't have absentee parents, so having the house to himself is a rarity. We all decided he needed to throw a party to celebrate.

"That's the plan."

Bentley gets a shit-eating grin on his face. "What if I told you I beat you to it?"

I narrow my eyes. "The fuck you say?"

"Why you getting so angry, bro?" The asshole laughs. "You say you're not into her. You told me you couldn't care less if I fucked her. If either of those things were true, why do you care who she goes to the party with?"

"I don't." I run my hands through my hair.

"Uh huh," he taunts. "Well, buddy, I'll do you a solid and admit that I haven't asked her... *yet*. But I *do* have every intention of making a move if you don't. You're not the only one she's hot for and I plan on exploiting the shit out of that."

This fucker is looking to get a rise out of me, but I won't let him.

I relax my jaw. "Be my guest."

He cocks his head to the side. "Is that your final answer?"

"Go for it," I insist. "Jasmine Callahan means nothing to me."

Bentley laughs. "All right, man, if you say so. But remember this conversation when she's in one of Reed's guest rooms with *me* on Friday night."

Not if I have anything to say about it.

chapter twenty-three

JAZZ

"You're going with me to Reed's party on Friday night."

I glance over at the bossy ass who just sat next to me at lunch. "Nice greeting, jackass. How about next time you try, 'Hi, Jazz. How's your day going?'"

Kingston's jaw clenches. I totally don't notice his eyes are more brown than green today. "Hi, Jazz. How's your day going?"

"See? That wasn't too hard, was it?" I give him a condescending pat on the cheek, making the rest of our table laugh.

"Watch it," he warns.

I lift my eyebrows in challenge. "Or what?"

He gives me a wicked grin. "Or I won't tell you about your surprise."

"*What* surprise?" Ainsley asks.

Kingston points to his sister. "Stay out of it, Ainsley."

She gives him a sugary smile before turning to me. "Do *you* want me to stay out of it, Jazz?"

I bite back a laugh. I love how much she enjoys fucking with her brother.

"Nope." I emphasize the word with a pop. "*What* surprise?"

Kingston stares at my lips before moving back up to my eyes.

"Go to Reed's party with me and I'll tell you."

Bentley, who's sitting on the other side of me, leans into my ear and whispers, "Make him work for it, baby girl."

I sit back in my chair. "What makes you think I'd have the desire to go to any party after what happened during the last one I attended?"

Kingston rolls his eyes. "Because this will be different."

"How so?"

He holds up his index finger. "For one, you'll be under our protection so no one will fuck with you." He adds a second finger. "Two, it's at Reed's house, so we have complete control over the environment." His ring finger joins in. "Three, it'd be a surefire way of getting back at Peyton and her groupies for bullying you."

Kingston looks so smug, I want to smack him.

"For one, being under your supposed protection doesn't stop *you* from screwing with me. I'm still convinced you had something to do with why I was so fucked up after only two drinks. Two, the location has *zero* influence over my decision because I don't trust you. See reason number one. And three, *you've* bullied me, so wouldn't refusing to go be getting back at you?" I tick off each reason mockingly.

A muscle jumps in Kingston's jaw. "You done?"

"Are you?" I challenge.

"Not even close." Kingston turns to Ainsley. "You're going, right?"

"Yeah." Ainsley looks at me. "You can ride with me if you want, Jazz. I swear I won't take off like I did last time. And if you don't want to drink, I won't either."

"Fine," I agree.

Going to a party with Ainsley has to be better than sitting at Sperm Donor's McMansion all night.

"Then it's settled. You'll ride with Ainsley and later in the evening, you'll be riding *me*." Bentley pulls me into his side.

I push him off. "You wish."

He winks. "Ain't denying that."

I smile, hating how much of a sucker I am for his charm. "Idiot."

"Ah, but you want me anyway," Bentley teases.

I smile wryly. "Nah. I'm not into bro dudes."

Bentley gasps dramatically. "You take that back! I am *not* a bro dude!"

I shrug. "If the douchebag fits..."

Bentley picks me up right out of my chair, setting

me on his lap. "Just for that, you can sit on my lap for the rest of lunch."

"Put me down, you jerk!"

I release an embarrassing squeal when he squeezes my leg right above the knee. I'm horribly ticklish there which Bentley quickly figures out. I laugh and squirm until I feel how I'm affecting him. The large thing poking me in the ass causes me to still *immediately*.

Bentley lifts his hips, ever so slightly, pressing his erection into my butt even more. "Careful, Jazz," he whispers into my ear. "Don't start something you're not willing to finish."

I swiftly scurry to my seat when he releases me and make the mistake of letting my eyes roam the rest of the dining room. Bentley and I definitely made a giant spectacle of ourselves. Ainsley and Reed are eyeing me with amusement, probably because my entire face is flushed. Kingston, however, couldn't possibly look more hostile. Nor could Peyton and her squad.

Great. Just great.

∼

Okay, one thing I will admit, rich kids know how to throw a party. Reed's house is easily ten thousand square feet, but the bottom level is packed with bodies. So much for controlling the environment—this place is a damn fire hazard. It's also a den of iniquity. There's a professional DJ, a bar supplying alcohol when not a single person here is over twenty-one, and multiple seating areas where couples are engaging in various levels of foreplay or using drugs.

"This place is lit!" Ainsley shouts.

She drags me through the open space, pointing out different areas, clearly knowing where she's going. Quite a few girls stop us along the way, offering superficial conversation punctuated by air kisses. Every single one of them eyes me curiously but doesn't say a word to me. I can tell Ainsley hates this crap, but she remains poised as if she's had a lot of practice doing it.

Finally, a genuine smile stretches across her face when she spots Reed sitting on a black leather couch in front of a huge TV, smoking a J. Bentley and Kingston are on gaming chairs next to the couch, their feet kicked up, playing Xbox.

Reed's entire demeanor changes when he sees Ainsley. He goes from looking impossibly bored to ecstatic, just like that.

He gets off the couch and pulls Ainsley into a side hug. "Hey. When did you get here?"

"A few minutes ago," she says with hearts in her eyes.

Damn, this girl's got it bad. I was so happy to hear Reed is going to man up and talk to Kingston about dating Ainsley. Hell, he might've done it already if the hardness to Kingston's jaw is any indication. He may not like it, but the fact that he's not trying to interfere right now is a good sign.

"Jazzy Jazz!" Bentley shouts. "Come sit on my lap and be my good luck charm. Davenport's kicking my ass."

"No amount of luck will prevent me from kicking your ass," Kingston taunts.

Ainsley and Reed take a seat on the couch, so I decide to do the same. "No thanks. I'm fine right here."

"You're no fun, girl." Bentley's lips form into a pout. "Where's your drink? You need to loosen up."

I show him my water bottle. "Right here. No alcohol for this girl tonight."

Bentley's jaw drops. "What?! No, that just won't do."

"It's true," Ainsley says. "Neither one of us are drinking tonight."

Reed takes a hit from his joint and holds it out to her. "You want some?"

Ainsley shrugs as she takes it from him. "Sure." She wraps her lips around it and coughs after inhaling too much smoke. When I give her a look she says, "What?"

I eye the joint in her hand. "Didn't we just say we're not getting fucked up?"

"No, we said we weren't *drinking*. Weed doesn't get you fucked up like liquor does. And it's totally natural." She holds the J out to me. "You in?"

Oh, why the hell not? She's right—I've never been unaware of what I was doing while smoking weed. True, it could be laced but I know Reed would never do that to Ainsley, especially with Kingston right here. There's no harm in sharing the same blunt.

"That's what I'm talking about!" Bentley throws the controller down and squeezes next to me on the couch.

I pass Bentley the joint after taking a hit of my own.

Kingston grabs some paper and a grinder off the side table and starts rolling his own. I snort, not surprised in the least that he's not willing to share with us. I hold my breath when his tongue peeks out to lick the paper. He's well versed in the art of rolling, even taking the time to use a thin skewer to create a passageway for the smoke to travel so it burns evenly. I've never been a heavy smoker, but my ex works at a dispensary. He has an obsession with rolling perfect blunts and felt it was necessary to pass on the knowledge.

God, why does Kingston have to be so pretty to look at? He has that whole rich asshole thing down to a T, which doesn't normally do it for me, but with him, it works. Tonight, he's wearing dark jeans that are no doubt designer and a t-shirt that's molded to his muscular chest so well, I'm sure it's tailored to fit him perfectly. He must have had a haircut after school because the fade is cleaned up and the top is a bit shorter. He hasn't said a word to me yet—he just watches me with those intense ever-changing eyes, like he's waiting me out.

After a few passes, I'm rocking a nice high, sinking back into the plush couch. Ainsley and Reed have moved to a back corner of the room, engaged in their own private conversation. I smile when her melodious laughter rings out and continues uncontrollably. Oh yeah, girlfriend is definitely a lightweight. Kingston is still brooding, staring me down from his chair. I refuse to acknowledge this little game of chicken we have going on, so I focus on chatting with Bentley instead.

I'm so relaxed, I don't even think to move Bentley's hand when it lands on my thigh.

"I like what you've got on here, Jazzy Jazz." I shiver when his deep voice rumbles in my ear as his fingers begin to climb. "It's understated, but sexy as fuck. You don't even need to try and you have the attention of practically every guy in this house."

I'm wearing a black tank, black ripped skinny jeans, and matching Chucks. Silver bangles circle each of my wrists, but that's the only accessory I have on. I didn't even bother doing something special with my hair or makeup—I'm sporting a high ponytail with just a little eyeliner and pink lip gloss. I figured I wasn't coming here to impress anyone. I'm here to support my friend and get out of that suffocating mansion.

"Not every guy." I snort. "Broody McGrumperson hasn't said a word to me."

Bentley runs the bridge of his nose along the nape of my neck. "That doesn't mean you don't have his attention. I'd bet my Porsche he's staring at us right now, looking a tad homicidal."

He's speaking directly into my ear and the music's turned up, so there's no way Kingston heard him. I hate myself for needing to know, but I *have* to look. When my eyes find his, sure enough, Kingston's doing exactly what Bentley had predicted.

My eyes roll back when Bentley presses his lips against my skin. "Shit, that feels good."

I'm definitely aware of my actions, but Mary Jane always makes me horny because I'm hyperaware of every little touch. Damn it, why didn't I think of that before I smoked?

Bentley smiles against the crook of my neck before taking my flesh between his teeth and biting down gently. I'm fairly certain a moan just escaped my lips. The hand that was on my thigh is now pressed against my cheek, turning me inward.

Our mouths are mere inches apart. Bentley searches my eyes and says, "I can make you feel even better if you'll let me."

Lord help me, but I'm curious enough to see where he's going with this. "How so?"

"Dance with me."

I blink twice. "Huh?"

I bite my lip when he smiles. The guy has a great smile. "I said, *dance with me.*"

Bentley stands up and pulls on my hand until I'm following his lead into the main throng of people. As we get to an area where about a dozen sweaty bodies are grinding against each other, the DJ switches the song to Halsey's "Gasoline".

Bentley's hard body moves behind mine and starts swaying to the beat. I close my eyes, dancing in time with the haunting and sexy rhythm. Bentley's hands grip my hips with bruising force while his lips repeatedly run the length of my neck. My body is warm and pliant against his. The erection at my back is persistent and its owner groans loudly when I push into it further, giving him the friction he's so obviously seeking. Something niggles in the recesses of my brain, telling me this is a very bad idea, but another more rebellious part tells me to run with it.

As the song ends, I open my eyes to find hazel ones locked onto mine. Alarms are blaring in my head, telling me to abort. Everything about Kingston is screaming malevolence right now. From his steely gaze to the hard set of his jaw. His rigid posture and clenching fists. If looks could kill, I'd be dead on the spot.

Another song begins, but I couldn't tell you what it is because I'm too busy freaking out.

Bentley leans into my ear, breaking the spell. "Kingston looks like he's about to devour you whole."

In my opinion, he looks more like he's about to *murder* me whole, although he's definitely giving off a predator vibe.

"Uh..."

Kingston's eyes briefly flicker over my shoulder before meeting my gaze and mouthing, *Run.*

I don't hesitate for even a second. I take off at full speed, slamming into grumbling bodies in my mission to flee. I dart down a hallway but quickly realize what a dumb move that was, so I turn around to head in the other direction. I stop dead in my tracks when I see the imposing man standing no more than ten feet away, coming closer with each long stride. Kingston's nostrils flare as his chest rises and falls rapidly. I counter each one of his steps with a backward retreat. I don't dare take my eyes off him, but I spy an open doorway in my peripheral, debating whether or not I'd have time to lock myself in there before Kingston catches up with me. I decide it's worth a shot since I'm running out of hallway.

Kingston reads my mind before I can make a move, so it's only a matter of seconds before rough hands are grabbing me, shoving me through the doorway. He slams the door shut behind him, locking us in a powder room. Damn it, why am I always getting stuck in bathrooms alone with this guy?

He unclenches his jaw before speaking. "You trying to get my attention, Jazz?"

I shake my head, willing my heart to calm its frantic beats. "What? *No.* Why would you think that?"

He crowds me against the counter and lifts a brow in challenge. "No? What did you not understand about the fact that you are *mine*? The way you were grinding up against my best friend says otherwise." His eyes darken. "You want us to share? Is that it?"

My fear is shifting into anger. Or arousal. Nope, let's go with anger.

"No, I do *not* want you to share!" Hopefully that

sounded a lot more convincing than it did in my head. "But for the record, what I do with my body is none of your business. Who I allow to touch me is *none of your business!* I am *not* yours!"

He grips the back of my neck, squeezing until I wince. "I don't fucking think so."

Kingston leans down until I'm forced to bend backward over the sink and slams his mouth against mine. I press my lips firmly together, denying his kiss, but then he bites my lower lip so hard, the metallic taste of blood seeps into my mouth when I gasp. Kingston wraps my ponytail around his fist, yanking my head back farther as his tongue pushes in. All pretenses of not wanting this leaves my body in a rush when the tip of his tongue glides against mine.

I slide my hands under his t-shirt, wrapping my arms around his torso. I pull Kingston into me, scratching my nails down his back. The faucet is digging into my spine and my damn lip is stinging. I desperately want him to feel the pain like I do. There's a tornado of conflicting emotions within me that should scare the shit out of me, but it doesn't. Instead, my body purrs in excitement, recognizing the same chaos within him. Our damaged souls call out to each other like a siren, solidifying this fucked up connection we seem to have.

I moan into his mouth when Kingston kicks my legs apart and grinds his hard-on into me. Every inch of my body is touching his as we drink each other in.

He and I have some pretty significant problems with one another, but that doesn't stop me from doing this. Kingston Davenport's touch seems to be the only thing that can make me not hurt so much, and I'm sick and tired of hurting so damn much.

He rips his mouth away when I stroke his dick through his jeans. "You owe me an apology. Getting on your knees and putting that sexy mouth on my dick is a great way to start."

"That's never going to happen." My laugh turns into a groan when Kingston plucks my hardened nipple. "The apology part."

He gives me a salacious grin. "But the blowjob part is on the table?"

If I wasn't already so flushed, I would be now. I bite my lip, debating my answer. Does the thought of working Kingston over with my mouth, knowing that I'm the one bringing him pleasure turn me on? Sure. But I don't like the thought of giving in to him so easily. Evidently, I'm taking too long to answer because he speaks up again.

"Fine. I'll go first—flip over. I want you to watch what I do to you in the mirror."

It takes me a second to catch up when he stands upright. Once the meaning of his words sinks in, I turn onto my stomach, resting it on the counter. Kingston turns my head until I'm facing a full-length mirror propped in the corner. It's one of those heavy old-fashioned ones that stands on its own.

"What are you—"

Kingston unbuttons my jeans. "Just shut the fuck up and watch."

I bristle at his rudeness, but when he slides my pants and underwear to my knees and crouches down to give me one long lick, I'm no longer offended. He wastes no time diving in, devouring me like I'm his last meal. I watch our reflection as Kingston sits on his knees, eating me from behind. He inserts one finger and then another, pumping in and out as he continues his assault on my clit. My moans are followed by his groans as he licks and sucks with just the right amount of pressure.

My legs are trapped by my clothing, so I don't have much room to move, even though I'm dying to. I kick off my left shoe and start clumsily pushing my pants down. Kingston gets the hint and yanks them the rest of the way until one leg is free. He switches positions, now slouching on the floor with his neck craned back. He removes his fingers from my pussy and wraps both arms around my thighs, pulling me down. I widen my stance, straddling his face, gripping the countertop for support.

"You taste so fucking good," he murmurs. "Better than I imagined."

I don't have time to wonder how many times he's fantasized about this because once he wraps his lips around my clit and sucks, an orgasm barrels down my spine, shocking the hell out of me with its intensity.

I've been trying to keep quiet this entire time, not wanting to alert anyone to what we're doing, but as I come, I scream Kingston's name.

With a nibble on my inner thigh, Kingston rises from the floor and locks eyes with me through the mirror. We're both flushed and a little sweaty. His dark blond hair is a complete disaster from all the face sitting, and his lips are shiny from my arousal. Someone's been banging on the door for who knows how long, complaining about a line building, so there's no way Kingston and I are walking out of this room without notice. With our disheveled state—and you know, the screaming orgasm—there's also no way they won't know what we were doing in here.

He presses his erection into me, holding my gaze. "We're not done here. We're not even *close* to done. I want you to think about that—and how hard you just came—the next time you want to lie to yourself, telling yourself you don't belong to me." Kingston tugs my ponytail aside and places a soft kiss right behind my ear. I can smell myself on him and for some sick reason, I'm even more turned on. "You're fucking *mine*, Jazz. You can fight it all you want, but that doesn't make it any less true."

I glare at his amused smirk as I quickly redress. He waits for me to finish, hand poised on the doorknob. The giant bulge in his pants is pretty hard to ignore, no pun intended. I hate that part of me feels guilty for leaving him high and dry yet again. I *really* despise the fact that an even bigger part feels deprived because I don't know what it feels like to have him inside of me.

I nod to it. "Are you going to at least try hiding that monster in your pants?"

"Not at all."

He turns the handle and opens the door. As he's stepping into the hallway, he adds, "By the way... that surprise I mentioned earlier. Be ready Sunday morning at ten. We have Belle for the day."

My jaw drops in shock as I watch him walk away without another word. I step out of the room to chase after him, but I freeze when I see the line of people hugging the wall outside of the bathroom. My face reddens as a girl shoves me out of the way, muttering something about almost peeing her pants while I was getting off. As I do my walk of shame down the hallway, most are smiling or chuckling at my expense. When I get to the end of the line, I see Peyton and Whitney scowling. What the hell are they doing here anyway? I had assumed Reed would keep them away after they cornered me at school.

"Slut," Peyton mutters as I pass.

I stop and turn to her. "Excuse me?"

She props a hand on her hip. "You heard me, *slut*. Don't act so self-righteous. Not when you're all over Bentley one minute and then fucking Kingston in the bathroom the next."

I refuse to let her get to me. I smile before leaning in and stage-whispering my next comment.

"Careful, Peyton. You're looking a little green and it's not really your color."

Her lips thin, but I don't wait around to hear anything else. When I get to the end of the hall, Bentley's standing there, having witnessed the interaction. He narrows his brown eyes in Peyton and Whitney's direction before turning them back to me.

"You okay?"

"I'm fine." I jerk my head over my shoulder. "I don't think they are though. Someone should probably escort them out before a tantrum ensues."

Bentley laughs. "You leave that to me, baby girl. Ains was just looking for you. You go catch up with her while I take out the trash."

As I head back to where I last saw Ainsley, I have a chilling thought. It wasn't that long ago when Kingston was referring to me as trash and now he's practically stamping his brand on my ass like a caveman.

I'm not sure which one is worse.

chapter twenty-four

KINGSTON

"Son, come in. Close the door behind you."

I walk into my dad's corporate office Monday after school. He's the CEO of Davenport Boating, a yacht manufacturing company he took over from my grandfather. As far as he knows, I plan on double majoring in business and law so I can take the reins when he retires. Considering the man is fifty-nine, I'd think that's scheduled to happen sometime in the next decade. What he doesn't know, is if I can pull this off, his golden years will be spent in a six-by-eight cell.

My father has his hands in several different businesses and not all of them legal. Running a Fortune 500 pays well but greedy fucker that he is, he can never procure enough wealth. I'm fairly certain money is the only reason he married my mother, who was the sole heir to a luxury hotel chain. God knows they were *nothing* alike. She was significantly younger than him yet somehow, he charmed her into bed and convinced her to marry him when she became pregnant with twins. Hell, I wouldn't be surprised if he knocked her up on purpose.

When she died, the only thing my dad inherited was a small savings account and a few vacation properties. My maternal grandfather had insisted she had an iron-clad prenup, equally dividing the bulk of her estate to any children she gave birth to. My father challenged the will, trying to find a loophole, but there were none. The only reason I know any of this is because my grandfather told me shortly before he died two years ago. He hated my father—never trusted him and right-fully so. Preston Davenport is one shady motherfucker.

I haven't brought any of this information to Ains-ley's attention yet. As far as she's concerned, our dad is cold, absent, and a habitual womanizer, but she has no idea what evils he's truly capable of. I know one day it will come to light, but I'm choosing to protect her naivety for the time being.

I shut the door and take a seat in front of his desk. "You wanted to see me? This couldn't wait until you got home?"

He shakes his head. "I'm heading straight to the airport after this. I just needed to drop in and check on a few things before I left town."

"Where are you going now?"

"Miami. The annual yacht show doesn't begin until

Friday, but there're industry professional events throughout the week. I figured it was a good time to spy on the competition."

I have no doubt he's heading to Miami. I do, however, highly doubt the reason behind this trip has anything to do with boats.

I nod. "Why am I here, Dad?"

The LA skyline is behind his back as he steeples his fingers. "I wanted to see how your little project with Jasmine Callahan is going."

"I have it handled."

He raises a salt-n-pepper brow. "You sure about that? I hear she's causing problems with her stepsister."

I clench my jaw. "*Peyton* is the one causing problems and I have that handled as well."

"You know..." My father twirls a pen between his fingers. "I have no problem with you sampling the merchandise, so to speak, but I hope you know better than to get emotionally involved with this girl."

"Who said I was emotionally involved?"

His greenish-brown eyes, identical to my own, assess me carefully. "I have my sources."

I scoff. "Well, your sources are *wrong*. I don't get emotionally involved. The only thing I want from a woman is her pussy."

A genuine smile lights up his over-Botoxed face. "Don't forget about their mouths or asses. Hell, even their tits, although the Callahan girl doesn't exactly have *those* assets."

I grit my teeth. I happen to love Jasmine's tits. Yeah, they're small, but they're perky and they fit her tiny frame. It's actually nice being with someone natural for a change. Shit, I'm pretty sure my sister and Jazz are the only girls at Windsor who didn't get a set of double-Ds for their sixteenth birthdays.

I bite back what I really want to say and instead, tell him what he wants to hear. "She doesn't need 'em. With her tight pussy, round ass, and plump lips, my dick has plenty of places to go. If I ever wanted to fuck a pair of big tits, I have plenty on standby."

My father releases a boisterous laugh. "That's my boy! You're right—she doesn't need the tits. I wouldn't mind taming that girl one bit just the way she is. Maybe you can throw her my way when you're done with her?"

I resist the urge to launch myself across this desk and punch the asshole. The sad thing is, this man has *no clue* how fucked up this conversation is between a man and his eighteen-year-old son.

I scrub a hand over my face, my tolerance wearing thin. "Is that all?"

He nods. "For now. Although, I feel I should remind you what's at stake here. You do well with this, Charles and I will introduce you to a world you could only dream of. Countless beautiful women, eager to please, and riches at your disposal. He and I aren't getting any younger, you know. We could use someone like you on our team."

I force myself to look bored with this conversation. "*What* team?"

He gives me a smarmy smile. "All in due time, son. All in due time."

~

A knock sounds at the door of my pool house. I check the time on my phone, surprised the pizza delivery guy is here already. When I open the door, my face falls. I was expecting a large pepperoni and olive. Instead, I get a tall, over enhanced blonde.

I block her entrance when she tries crossing the threshold. "What do you want, Vanessa?"

My father's wife trails her French-manicured nail down my chest. "Your father's gone."

I remove her hand when she goes for my belt. "So?"

Vanessa pushes her shoulders back, which causes her tits to jut forward. She's wearing a sheer, light pink nightie with no panties. It's pretty obvious why she's here right now, but I enjoy making her squirm.

"So..." She goes for my belt again and this time, I take a step back, causing her to pout. "I thought we could have a little fun. I miss you, baby."

I scoff. "Save the pet names for your sugar daddy. I'm not interested."

Vanessa scrunches her nose. "What do you mean you're not interested?"

Contrary to popular belief, I'm not one to stick my

dick into any willing pussy. Shit, I didn't even do more than kiss Ariana at that party. I told her to moan for me so Jazz would make assumptions and she didn't even question it before putting on a porn-worthy show.

"Kingston? Did you hear me?"

My eyes leisurely roam Vanessa's body. My dad's wives get younger and younger with each marriage. Vanessa's twenty-two and practically lives in our home gym, so her body is fit and firm in all the right places. She's the only woman I've fucked since Peyton, although I allow Peyton to believe otherwise. When Vanessa heard that Peyton and I had broken up, she came over to tell me how sorry she was, by swallowing my cock.

The woman is hot and she fucks like a pro, but if I'm being honest, the only reason I even took her up on her offer was to screw over my dad. Vanessa's nothing but a trophy to him—that's common knowledge—but Preston Davenport expects monogamy from his wives, despite the fact that he never lives up to it on his end. His ego is far too fragile to have a woman cheat on him, which is why he's on his fourth marriage.

The delivery guy walks up behind Vanessa, eyes wide when he sees she's practically naked. I pull a fifty out of my pocket and hand it to him in exchange for the pizza.

"Thanks, man." His eyes are still on my stepmother.

I nod to the pizza guy, but I'm speaking to Vanessa. "If you want to shove someone's cock down your throat so bad, I'm sure this guy would be more than willing."

"Uh..." said guy stammers. "Yeah... sure. You want me to whip it out right here?"

Vanessa looks over her shoulder before turning back to me. "Is that what gets you off, Kingston? You want to watch me blow someone else?"

I set the pizza box down and lean against the door-jamb. "Oh yeah. It would turn me right the fuck on. Maybe if you do a good enough job, we can see how sexy you look being spit-roasted."

She smiles and immediately drops to her knees in front of the delivery guy. My tone couldn't have possibly been more sarcastic, but Vanessa Davenport isn't exactly the brightest crayon in the box.

The delivery guy hastily undoes his pants, pushing them down to his knees and Vanessa wastes no time hoovering his dick into her mouth.

He groans. "Jesus, this is my favorite porn fantasy come true."

I laugh as I start to close the door, but Vanessa releases him with a pop and says, "Where are you going? I thought you wanted to watch."

"Nah." I shake my head. "My pizza's getting cold. Besides, if you've seen one whore suck a cock, you've seen them all." The poor guy's boner is just hanging in the breeze, so I decide to do him a solid. "But... if my new friend here tells me you got him off real good, I might let you blow me next."

I wait until she sucks his dick back into her mouth before closing the door and turning the lock. I have zero intention of letting that dumb bitch ever touch my cock again, but at least the delivery guy will get to bust a nut. And if someone happens to leave a flash drive with the footage from my security feed on my father's desk, so be it. Call it my good deed for the year.

chapter twenty-five

JAZZ

"You get a homecoming dress yet?" Kingston asks.

I roll my eyes. He won't stop bugging me about this stupid dance.

"I'm not going. I'm not sure which part of that statement is so confusing for you."

Ainsley gasps. "What? Jazz! You *have* to go to homecoming! It's our senior year! Homecoming is one of the only things I actually enjoy in this school. It's fun getting all dressed up for the night."

"*I* don't think it's fun getting dressed up for the night." Bentley winks at me. "But I would for you, babe. Then after the dance, we can get *undressed* together."

I don't miss the way Kingston's eyes narrow in disapproval at his best friend. It's been a week since Reed's party and Bentley hasn't backed off on the flirting one bit. I swear he's doing it to fuck with

Kingston, who is still being a complete Neanderthal. With the exception of our outing with my sister last weekend, I've been avoiding alone time with him. Ainsley's been driving me to school and Frank takes me home, despite Kingston's protests, so we only see each other during lunch, like right now, and in Lit class. I know it's only a matter of time before he bulldozes me, but I'm enjoying the reprieve.

I give Bentley a wry look. "As sweet as the offer is, Bentley, I'm still gonna pass."

"That doesn't work for me," Ainsley whines. "C'mon, Jazz, you have to go—it's the best part of the week. You need to say yes and then we need to bust ass to find you the perfect dress. I'm sure the racks are practically empty by now since we have just over two weeks until homecoming."

"What about the lake house?" Reed asks. "Now, *that's* the best part."

She giggles. "Well, that's a given. But I want to wear a pretty dress and dance before that."

My brows pinch together. "*What* lake house?"

Bentley lays his arm over my shoulders. "There's a tiny little mountain town about ninety minutes away. It has a big lake and badass log cabins. We party it up until the next day. Lots of booze, weed, and general debauchery. Three of my favorite things."

"For fuck's sake." I stash his comment about debauchery in the back of my mind. "Who's *we*?"

Kingston pushes Bentley's arm away and hooks

his foot under my chair, pulling me closer to him. "Ains, Reed, Bent, and I always stay in my family's cabin."

"That's it?" I ask. "Just you guys?"

Ainsley speaks up when her brother remains silent. "Give her the whole story, dickwad."

He flips her off. "Your dad also owns a cabin up there; it's right next to ours."

"So, Peyton will be there," I surmise.

Kingston nods. "Yes, but so will a lot of other people. *And* she knows not to fuck with you."

"We'll see how long that lasts," I mutter.

He jerks his head toward Peyton's table. "See? She's not even looking over here. She's probably pretending you don't exist. If Peyton knows what's good for her, she'll keep it that way."

She *has* been doing that. I've run into her a few times at the house this week and every time, she heads in the opposite direction the moment she sees me. It doesn't stop her from sending scathing looks my way or muttering insults under her breath, but she *is* physically staying away. Something tells me she's just biding her time though. A girl like her doesn't give up that easily. Unless...

I tilt my head to the side. "Did you *hurt* her?"

"*No*, I didn't hurt her." Kingston scoffs. "Jesus, thanks for your vote of confidence. I didn't *do* anything. I just reminded her that if she or any of her minions fucked with you, I'd take that as a personal attack on me. Peyton may act obtuse sometimes, but she's not stupid. None of them are."

I chew on that for a moment. "I don't have money to spend on a dress and I'm sure as shit not about to ask Daddy Warbucks. I'll go to the lake but not the dance."

"I'll cover the dress," Kingston grumbles. "And whatever the fuck else you need. Consider it a birthday present."

My mouth gapes. "How do you know about that?"

Kingston gives me a look that says, *Really?*

"Wait," Ainsley interjects. "When's your birthday?"

"The day of the dance," Kingston answers.

"September twenty-fifth," I reply at the same time.

Ainsley's eyes widen. "We'll celebrate your birthday at the lake! I'll get you a cake and everything."

Kingston speaks quietly against my ear. "We have a standing date with your sister—every Sunday unless you say otherwise. We can come back from the lake early, pick her up, and spend the day in Santa Monica if you want."

Tears prick at my eyes. I was expecting to spend my birthday weekend alone, being consumed by grief. Now, I had two people offering to make my mom's absence a little less painful. How can I say no to that?

I sigh. "Okay, I'm in."

Ainsley claps her hands excitedly. "We should all go to the dance together!"

"I'm good with that." Reed takes a bite of his pizza.

"Me too. But only if Jazzy Jazz saves *lots* of room for me on her dance card." Bentley glances at Kingston and smirks. "We all know how much she *loves* dancing with me."

I throw a fry at Bentley's face. "Asshat."

He blows me a kiss in response.

"Fine," Kingston grumbles.

"Awesome!" Ainsley says. "It's settled then. Jazz, I don't have rehearsal on Fridays, so we'll go shopping after school."

Okay then. I guess I'm going to homecoming.

∼

Well, today's the day. Homecoming. Also, the day I'm officially considered a legal adult.

Sperm Donor is out of town again—no surprise there—but he did shock me by having Ms. Williams deliver a birthday gift. Normally, I wouldn't feel comfortable accepting anything from him, especially knowing he's not the man he'd like the general public to believe he is. I still don't know exactly what's going on there, but Kingston promised he'd tell me everything soon.

That said, Charles' gift is actually something useful and as much as I hate to admit... thoughtful. He paid for driving lessons so I can get my license. A brand new black Audi SUV is sitting in the garage with my name on it—booster seat included—just waiting for me to pass the test. I already called them and set up my first lesson. The sooner I get my license, the sooner I'll be able to get to Belle without relying on someone else.

A month ago, I would've been plotting my escape from the Callahan estate. But now... now I don't think it's all that bad. Don't get me wrong, that house is colder than the arctic. Charles is never around, Peyton is... well, Peyton. And ever since Madeline found out that Kingston and I have been hanging out, she's not nearly as friendly as she was initially. I'm perfectly okay with their lack of warmth though. I have no need for fake or selfish people in my life.

Belle, Ainsley, and even the guys, are enough. Over the last two weeks, things have been... good. Peaceful. Not a single attempt to harass me has been made. After school, sometimes I watch Ainsley rehearse, but other times, I hang out with the guys. They may come across as irredeemable assholes, but when they're together outside of school, they're really just normal teenage guys. They eat *all the time*, play video games, watch sports, party, or just chill. There's a brotherhood between them that's endearing—they're fiercely loyal to one another. All three of them have an obvious soft spot for Ainsley and somehow, that's extended to me as well, especially with Kingston.

He and I have taken Belle out four different times now and each time, he weasels his way into my heart a little farther. He makes it easy to forget the way he treated me when we first met or the secrets he's still keeping.

Watching Kingston with Belle is truly a thing of beauty. He's so sweet to her and she absolutely adores him. Kingston finally admitted that he pays Jerome for our weekly visits. While I'm annoyed at Belle's dad for being such a selfish ass, I'm thankful Kingston thought of it. Kingston says there's not much money can't buy and I'm beginning to see the truth in that.

"Holy shit, chica, you look fucking hot!" Ainsley wiggles her eyebrows for effect. "My brother and Bentley are going to have major boners all night."

I shake my head. "Thanks... I think."

I take in my reflection and smile. I couldn't have imagined a more perfect dress. The satin bodice has a heart-shaped neckline with spaghetti straps and a lace overlay. The chiffon skirt is flirty and flouncy, hitting me about mid-thigh. The eggplant color complements my bronzed skin beautifully and the gold sparkly sandals I'm wearing completes the look. Ainsley styled my hair in a half updo with the long pieces curled down my back. She topped it off with the smoky eye, pink lip makeup combo, giving the whole thing a sultry, but classy vibe.

I mimic her eyebrow movements. "You're looking pretty fine yourself, lady."

Ainsley's dress is similar in style to mine but hers is bright red and backless. Reed is going to be speechless. She looks absolutely stunning.

She loops her arm through my elbow. "We should ditch the guys and just go together. We'd make a hot couple. I'd totally bang you. You know, if I was into chicks."

I laugh. "Ditto."

A quick knock sounds on her bedroom door before it opens. "Ains, the limo's here. You re—"

Kingston stands in the doorway, swallowing hard as his eyes travel the length of my body. Mine do the same to him. Twice. Goddamn, he looks good in a well fitted suit. Like, unfairly so. I don't miss the fact that his tie happens to match my dress. He hasn't seen it before now, so Ainsley must've told him what color to wear.

"Fuck," he mutters under his breath.

My brows crinkle. "Is that a good 'fuck' or a bad 'fuck'?"

"I'm fairly certain there's no such thing as a bad fuck where you're concerned, Jazz." Kingston's eyes darken as he rubs a hand over his jaw. "Care to test out my theory?"

Shit. It's been weeks since he's touched me sexually and my lady bits are pretty salty about that. There's only so many times I can give myself a mediocre orgasm before it's just not worth the effort. If Kingston didn't look like he wanted to devour me at all times, I'd be concerned he's lost interest. That's clearly not the case but part of me wonders why he hasn't even *attempted* to touch me since that night in Reed's bathroom. Granted, we haven't been alone often but there's definitely been opportunity. I almost made a move several times but then I wondered if he was getting it from someone else. Maybe he's not touching me because someone else is keeping him satisfied. I can't lie to myself anymore and say the thought of that doesn't bother me.

"God, you guys, get a room and just get it over with. I can't handle being around the world's longest eye fuck anymore."

Kingston ignores his sister, crossing the room until he's standing right before me. Leaning into my ear, he says, "You look fucking incredible in this dress but fair warning: I plan on ripping it off your body as soon as possible."

I'd like to say his words don't affect me, but sadly, I cannot. I'm pretty sure I whimper as chills scatter down my spine.

"You wish." My words come out breathy.

Kingston pulls back, lips curling in amusement. "Don't pretend I'm the only one, princess."

"Ugh!" Ainsley whines. "Seriously, guys. Gross. I don't need to witness your foreplay."

He crosses the room again, stopping just outside the doorway. "Get a move on. The guys are downstairs and the limo's waiting out front."

It takes me a few seconds to gather my wits before I'm following him and Ainsley down the curved staircase. When we reach the ground level, Bentley and Reed are standing there smiling, looking sexier than ever. Reed only has eyes for Ainsley, but Bentley makes no effort to conceal the fact that he's drinking me in *real* slowly.

Bentley whistles. "Damn, baby girl. You look *good*."

He's also wearing a dark suit and looks just as delicious as Kingston in his. I bite my lip when Kingston stands next to Bentley, and now I have both of their gazes drilling into me. Dear Lord, the pheromones, or whatever they're giving off, are *potent*.

Ainsley slips her hand through Reed's crooked elbow as I join Kingston and Bentley.

I finger the lapel to Bentley's suit jacket. "Looking pretty dapper there, Bent. You clean up well."

He bends his elbow, but Kingston pulls me back before I can take Bentley's proffered arm.

"Hey!" I gripe.

Bentley laughs and holds his palms out in the universal sign for *chill the fuck out, dude*.

Kingston leans into my ear and growls, "Don't fucking test me right now. I'm already having a hard enough time knowing every asshole at that dance will be checking you out."

I roll my eyes. "Stop being such a damn alphahole."

Kingston runs the bridge of his nose up my neck, making my breath hitch. "Stop being so fucking stubborn and just do what I say."

Well, now I want to do the exact opposite. You'd think he'd know by now how little I appreciate being bossed around.

I push off of Kingston and grab Bentley's arm. "C'mon, handsome. Let's get to that dance so you can spin me around the floor a few times."

Bentley's smile takes over his face. "Anything you say, baby girl."

chapter twenty-six

JAZZ

The homecoming dance is being held at a fancy hotel in downtown Los Angeles. Bentley and I walk into the ballroom arm-in-arm, much to Kingston's annoyance. Screw him. If he wants to sulk like a child, I'm not going to let him ruin my night. It's not only my birthday but this is also my first high school dance and now that I'm here, I plan on making the most of it.

My old school didn't have money for things like this. There was no homecoming dance and prom wasn't a big event because not many people had enough money to buy formal wear. It would've *never* been held in a five-star hotel like this. Hell, they barely had enough funding to decorate the school's outdated gym. Spending the evening in a room that smelled like sweaty feet while dressed in clothing you couldn't afford wasn't all that appealing.

My eyes widen as I take in the space. The lighting is low with fairy lights on every available surface, glinting off the chandeliers up above. A large dance floor is surrounded by round tables adorned with white tablecloths and tall floral centerpieces. Along the side wall, there're refreshments, and the back wall has a stage and DJ booth. It's really pretty; the whole place has sort of an ethereal glow to it.

"C'mon, baby girl. Let's dance." Bentley drags me to the dance floor, not waiting for a response.

The tempo is fast, so we remain a respectable distance apart as we dance from one song to the next. Out of the corner of my eye, I occasionally spot Kingston leaning against the wall scowling, but I refuse to let him ruin this for me. Ainsley and Reed join in at one point and we switch partners for a bit until the DJ finally announces he's slowly things down. Bentley pulls me close as Rihanna's "Love on the Brain" begins belting through the speakers.

"You having fun, birthday girl?"

I nod. "I am."

Bentley looks over my shoulder before sliding his hands perilously close to my ass. "Have I told you how fucking beautiful you look tonight?"

"You have." I smile shyly. "More than once."

Bentley leans down and nuzzles his nose against my cheek. "I meant it, and as fun as this has been, it looks like my dawg's patience has snapped."

Before I can ask any follow-up questions, I'm pulled

out of Bentley's arms into a solid chest. My body instantly recognizes who it's up against. I have to stifle a moan at the feeling of his hard body pressed against mine. Bentley winks before walking away, leaving me at Kingston's mercy. As Rihanna sings about fist fighting with fire just to get close to someone, his hands bracket my hips.

Kingston presses his mouth against my ear. "I'm done playing bullshit games with you, Jazz."

My breath catches as he starts grinding into me from behind. "Who said I'm playing games?"

His teeth clamp down on the spot where my neck meets my shoulder, making me simultaneously gasp and wince. He never answers my question and, instead, grabs my hand, pulling me out of the ballroom.

"What are you doing?" I try jerking away from him, but it's no use.

Kingston's head snaps back. "Just shut the fuck up before I throw you over my shoulder."

I'm too shocked—and turned on by that image—to do anything but follow. He turns the handle on a few different doors before finding one that's unlocked. Kingston whips the door open and shoves me into a darkened room.

My eyes don't even have time to adjust before he's on me, crashing his lips against mine. A palpable need consumes us as our tongues battle for supremacy. Kingston rips his mouth away, leaving a trail of kisses down my neck as he kneads my breast. My hands find the zipper of his pants, sliding it down while his are pawing the back of my dress.

"Where the fuck is the zipper on this thing?"

"Left side," I pant.

He finds the hidden zipper, yanking it down before pushing the straps off my shoulders. My bra is off in a flash, and his tongue immediately finds my nipple, circling the tightened bud before sucking it into his mouth.

My head falls back. "Oh, shit."

I push Kingston's suit jacket off while his nimble fingers work the buttons of his shirt. Once his bare chest is exposed, I slide my nails down the ridges of his chest and abdomen before pulling his dick out of his pants and pumping my fist up and down.

Kingston releases a strangled groan. "Fuck."

I step out of the dress, pooling at my feet. My eyes have adjusted enough where I can see the whites of his eyes widen as I drop to my knees before him. I pull Kingston's pants down over his hips and, without preamble, suck the flared head into my mouth. My nails bite into his ass as I bob up and down before opening my jaw and lowering farther. Kingston releases a string of curses as I swallow, bringing him into my throat. He groans as I pull back, flattening my tongue on the underside of his cock before releasing him with a pop.

"Fucking hell, Jazz," Kingston mutters.

Before I can dive back in, Kingston scoops his

hands under my armpits and lifts me up. He taps the back of my thighs, prompting me to jump as he lifts me up, circling my legs around his waist.

A smirk toys at my lips. "What's wrong? You're not a fan of deep throating?"

He takes a few steps forward before setting me down on the edge of a conference table.

"That was quite possibly my favorite thing ever, but I'd be a two-pump chump if you kept that up."

The laughter dies on my lips as he pulls my underwear to the side, exposing my pussy to the air-conditioned room. Kingston wastes no time, his fingers honing in on my entrance and dipping inside. He curls his fingers and starts rubbing his thumb over my clit. I start riding his hand, furiously trying to get there when he stops abruptly.

"Hey!" I whine. "What the hell are you doing? Move, goddammit!"

"You're not in control here, sweetheart. The sooner you figure that out, the better."

I know that's not exactly true. If I told him I wasn't ready to have sex, he'd respect that. He'd be pissed, considering how worked up we both are, but he wouldn't force himself on me. I have absolutely no intention of telling him to stop, though. If he keeps working his magical fingers, I can pretend for a bit.

I wrap my fist around the tie still knotted at his neck. "Kiss me."

His white teeth flash in the darkness as a smile breaks out. "Say, please."

I narrow my eyes. "Bite me."

Kingston's teeth clamp down on the muscle running along the nape of my neck. I didn't mean that literally, but I'm not complaining.

My head falls back when his mouth lands on my nipple again, frantically flicking his tongue over one, then the other.

"Oh, God."

Kingston adds a third finger and increases his pace. "Your pussy is so tight and wet. I can't wait to get inside of you."

My eyes roll back in pleasure. "So do it already."

He removes his fingers and fumbles around for a moment before I hear a foil package being torn open. I watch the shadowed movements of his hand, sheathing his cock before I feel him against me. Kingston slides himself over my clit a few times before driving into me in one fell swoop.

"Motherfuck." Kingston pulls out and slams back into me more forcefully. "So. Fucking. Tight."

"Harder," I moan.

"Fuck, yes," he groans.

Kingston circles both of my ankles with his fingers and repositions them on his shoulders. He's so much deeper at this angle, it borders on the precipice between pleasure and pain. Neither one of us are worried about volume as he picks up the pace.

My back bows. "So close. So fucking close."

"Let me see you rub that pretty clit," he coos. "I want to watch as you get off all over my cock."

My fingers snake between us and start rubbing vigorously, tension building with each slip and slide. Only a few thrusts later, I'm coming harder than I ever have in my life.

"Fuck," Kingston groans. "That's it, baby. Come all over me. You feel so fucking good. You look so fucking perfect lying beneath me."

After my tremors wane, he leans forward, pushing my knees to my chest, my heeled sandals framing his ears. Kingston pumps into me with abandon until he's roaring through his own release. As he shudders against me, he places a single kiss on my sweaty temple.

"There's no getting away from me now, Jazz. I'll fucking kill anyone who tries taking you away from me."

The conviction in that statement should be terrifying, yet... I find myself smiling. Right now, I'd be pretty stabby too if someone tried pulling us apart. Kingston kisses down my jaw as we catch our breath, repeating the same word over and over.

"*Mine.*"

chapter twenty-seven

JAZZ

"So..." Ainsley spares me a quick glance as she drives. "Are you going to tell me why you needed to change your underwear before we took off?"

Shit. My overnight bag was in Ainsley's trunk. My panties were uncomfortably wet after Kingston and I were together. I had to get a new pair before we drove for an hour and a half to the lake. My dress is too short to risk going without anything. One slight breeze, and I would've been flashing my hoo-ha to the world. I thought I was discreet, but apparently not.

"Do I have to?"

"No... but how about you tell me where my brother dragged you off to? Or what you were doing for so long? Or why when you came back, you both had major sex hair?"

I side-eye her. "For the same reason I needed new

underwear. Do you really want details? He's your brother. Wouldn't that gross you out?"

"I didn't want a play-by-play, Jazz. But your non-answer gives me all the answer I need. Happy Birthday to *you*." She laughs. "Holy shit, I wish you could've seen the look on Peyton's face when they named Kingston homecoming king and he wasn't there. I swear to God, it looked like her head was going to literally explode as she stood up on that stage with her pretty crown, without her king. It was no secret he was off some-where with you. Hell, he practically clubbed you over the head in front of everyone."

I throw my head back against the seat. "Oh, God. It was that obvious?"

"*Totally* obvious."

I groan. "Crap. This party is going to be a shit show, isn't it?"

"Nah," she assures me. "If people are being nosy assholes, we can hide in the house and nosh on your birthday cake until we put ourselves in a sugar coma."

Ooh, I forgot about the birthday cake. I *love* cake.

"Can we do that anyway?"

"Let's see how it goes. You can't get the scenery or the lack of civilization in LA. You'll have fun; I promise."

I sigh. "I'm holding you to that."

"Here we are. C'mon, let's drop our bags inside."

Ainsley's Lambo comes to a stop and she shifts it into park. There's a bunch of cars here already. I spot

Bentley's and Reed's but I don't see either one of Kingston's yet. He said he had a few stops to make along the way, but that it shouldn't take too much time. He was being cryptic, so I suspect it may have something to do with the birthday present he mentioned earlier. I don't want to text him in case he's driving, so I get out of the car and follow Ainsley.

As soon as we step inside, my jaw drops when I see the large A-framed windows that make up the back end of the house. I can't see behind the people who are hanging on the deck, but Ainsley said the house is right on the lake. I bet the view is incredible during the day. Surprisingly, no one is inside, so I ask Ainsley about it.

"The main part of the house is off-limits to partygoers. There's a small boathouse they have access to, but... unless you're into group sex, stay away from it."

My eyes widen. "Seriously?"

"Seriously. We keep the music up loud to drown out the noises. As the night wears on, you'll see more and more people heading in that direction. Thankfully, our cabins are the only ones for miles, so neighbors aren't an issue."

I scrunch my nose. "Have any of the guys... uh, participated in the boathouse activities?"

She mimics my expression. "Not Kingston or Reed. Bentley... probably. I've never been in there, so I haven't actually *seen* him participating, but I *have* seen him go inside for the last two years. I wouldn't be shocked one bit if he ended up there tonight."

I take a moment to digest that. I can't say I'm surprised about Bentley joining a giant orgy. But I am... well, I don't know what I am. Disappointed maybe? A little skeeved out? Curious?

My brows draw together. "Where do the people not participating in an orgy sleep?"

"A lot of them take over Peyton's house. Or... your dad's house, technically. The rest sleep in the cabin next to it. It's a vacation rental that someone reserves during homecoming weekend."

"So, only you and the guys sleep here? Really? There's so much space."

Ainsley nods. "Well, and *you*. Kingston's really protective of this place, so he deemed it a no-go zone from the beginning. People can hang on the back deck, or anywhere on the property really, but not inside. He keeps everything locked up tight." She gets a sad smile on her face. "Our mom inherited this cabin from her grandparents and left it to us when she died. I think Kingston wouldn't care nearly as much if it were our dad's."

"Oh."

She jerks her head to the staircase on our right. "The bedrooms are up there. Let's put our bags away and we can head out back."

There're four bedrooms and two bathrooms on the upper level. Ainsley opens the door to each room and stops when we get to the master.

I peek inside. "Is this us?"

There's a four-poster king-sized bed in the center of the room with a matching wooden dresser and nightstand. The room is decent in size but the furniture takes up a lot of space.

"This is where my brother usually sleeps. I figured you might want to stay in here."

I don't know why, but my cheeks flush. "Uh... we haven't really discussed it. Can I drop my bag in our room and figure out sleeping arrangements later?"

She chuckles. "Sure, Jazz. Although, if I know my brother, he's not going to let you out of his sight."

We make our way into a smaller room at the opposite end of the hall. Ainsley and I set our bags inside the door.

I finger the hem of my dress. "Do you think we should change?"

"You can if you want, but I'm leaving this on for a while. It'll get chilly out there, but there's always a fire going in the pit. Plus, alcohol warms you up, and I plan on drinking plenty of that." She laughs. "Reed couldn't stop checking me out tonight, telling me how much he loved my dress. I'm hoping when I take it off, *he'll* be taking it off for me."

My eyebrows raise. "You're ready to take that step, huh?"

"Girl, I've been ready to take that step with Reed Prescott for *years*. Tonight, I might actually have a chance." She wags her eyebrows. "Especially if you're keeping my brother occupied, so help a sister out, will ya?"

Heat rushes through my body when I remember the last thing Kingston said to me before we walked back into the dance.

"Don't change before you go to the lake house. I plan on delivering on that promise to rip that dress off your body later."

I shake my head, clearing the memory. "Uh... I think I'll leave mine on too for now."

Ainsley laughs as if she's reading my mind. "Let's head out back and grab some drinks."

We step out onto a raised deck filled with people from school. I lean over the railing, squinting my eyes to see in the darkness. A large lake sits before us, the outdoor lighting reflecting off its smooth surface.

"This place is the shit."

Ainsley joins me at the railing, handing me a cup filled with slushy liquid. "Wait until you see it in the morning. I love it here."

I take a drink from my cup. "Damn, this is good. It tastes like a Jolly Rancher."

"Redneck margaritas, baby." Ainsley clinks her cup to mine. "I know it doesn't taste like it, but there's a shit ton of tequila in there so be careful."

"Noted." I nod. "Have you seen the guys yet?"

She shakes her head. "Not yet. They're probably down below barbequing or in the hot tub."

I take another sip from my drink. "You wanna head down there and check it out?"

Ainsley holds her index finger up. "Hold on. Let me top these drinks off then we can go."

She pulls the lanyard holding the house key off her neck and unlocks the door. I follow her inside to the open kitchen and wait as she grabs a pitcher out of the refrigerator and refills our drinks.

"Thanks," I say as I take the cup from her.

She jerks her head to the fridge. "Make sure you only drink from there. We're keeping the doors locked but if you want another, just let me know and I'll take care of you."

"Got it."

Ainsley grins widely. "Now, let's get back out there and enjoy this party!"

chapter twenty-eight

JAZZ

Man, you don't get fresh air like this in the city. I close my eyes and inhale deeply, breathing in the earthy pines. Ainsley's snuggling by the fire with Reed and Bentley is in the hot tub with a few other people I don't know. I didn't feel like joining Bent or being the third wheel, so I've been walking along the water, waiting for Kingston to get here. It's almost one in the morning, and the bastard still hasn't shown. I'd be worried at this point if Bentley hadn't already told me Kingston texted, saying he would be here shortly.

Drunken giggles draw my attention to a couple up ahead. They're walking down the small dock—stumbling, really—before reaching the boathouse and stepping inside. I look behind me and still no sign of Kingston, so I follow them. There's no way in hell I'm going inside, but I am curious enough to peek through the windows that are only covered by sheer panels.

"Holy shit."

The interior of the boathouse is made up of one big room with minimal furnishings, so there's not much blocking my view. The space is filled with two dozen or so naked bodies engaging in one sexual act or another. Moaning and groaning assaults my ears, interspersed with the occasional, "Oh, God!"

It seems no type of coupling is off-limits. I even spot one male-male-female-female train that's impressively well-coordinated. Jesus, this is insane. It's also virtually impossible for me to look away. I'm absolutely stunned, but also... excited. I can feel my nipples hardening and the sudden wetness in my panties. My blood thrums, and my pulse spikes as my eyes bounce from one live-action porn to another.

"You wanna go inside?"

I swear I jump a foot off the ground. *"Jesusmotherof-shit!"* I smack Bentley's chest. "You scared the crap out of me!"

His eyes twinkle. "Just when I thought you couldn't get any hotter, I find out you're a dirty little voyeur."

"I am *not* a dirty little voyeur!" I whisper-shout.

He leans into the window and takes a peek. "No? A regular voyeur then?"

I roll my eyes. "Oh my God, will you just shut up?"

Bentley smiles. "You know, Jazzy Jazz, if you wanted a closer look, I'd be more than happy to accompany you. Kingston would kick my ass, but it'd totally be worth it."

I start speed walking back toward solid ground. "You're an idiot."

He follows me and swings an arm over my shoulders. "And *you*, my dear, are a dirty birdy. *So hot*."

I shrug him off and cross my arms over my chest. "Speaking of Kingston... is he here yet?"

Bentley nods slowly. "Just arrived. I'm supposed to lead you to the little private birthday celebration he has lined up."

"It's after midnight, so it's technically not my birthday anymore."

He produces a blunt and lights up. "C'mon, baby girl. Take a walk with me."

"Fine," I huff. "But you're sharing that."

He passes the joint to me. "I wouldn't dream of it any other way."

I take a hit and exhale slowly. "Where are we going?"

Bentley tips his chin. "Up that way a bit."

I'm thankful I had the sense to change into flip-flops instead of trying to navigate the slightly damp terrain in heels.

"You got out of the hot tub just for this, huh?"

His lips turn up at the corners. "Nah. I got out of the hot tub when I saw you heading for the boathouse. You know, the place where you were *not* spying on people fucking."

303

Shit. I didn't think anyone was paying attention to what I was doing.

I point my finger at him. "If you ever repeat that, I swear to God, I will have your balls."

He laughs, ruining the smoke rings he was blowing. "Aw, baby girl. You already have me by the balls. But I wouldn't say no if you'd like to suck on them."

I smack his arm. "Jesus, do you ever quit?"

Bentley shrugs. "I don't know. Never had to really work for it before."

I sigh. "You know that whatever happened in that pool house will never happen again, right?"

"Never say never." He winks.

"What exactly *did* happen that night?"

Damn, I can't believe I didn't think to ask him before now. Bentley's way more forthcoming than Kingston.

He bumps his arm into mine. "Nothing. Well, besides the really hot making out you saw on that video."

I sigh. I knew there was little chance I slept with them that night, but it's a relief knowing for sure.

My brows furrow. "Then... why? And why do I have such little memory of it?"

"Now those are questions for my dawg. I'm not even touching that." He passes the joint back to me. "Chill, baby girl. It's your birthday weekend. You can worry about the heavy shit on Monday."

I take another drag, really feeling the buzz on that one. "How much farther?"

We've been walking for at least twenty minutes now. The sounds and lights from the party faded a while ago. Thankfully, the moon is full, so we have a decent amount of light since we're walking along the shore and not under the trees.

Bentley stops. "We're here."

I look around, but there's no sign of Kingston. Only another dock with a small speedboat tethered to it and an empty picnic table.

"Uh... this is nice and all, but wasn't Kingston supposed to meet us here?"

He pulls his phone out of his pocket and runs his thumbs over the screen. "Have a seat, babe. He was grabbing your cake and some drinks. He'll be right down."

I take a seat and pat the bench beside me. "I won't bite."

"Nah, I've done my job. I don't really wanna be here when your boy arrives. I'm gonna head back to the boathouse, although I'm much more of a doer than a watcher." He wags his eyebrows.

I shake my head. "Ugh, I didn't need to know that."

Bentley shrugs. "Quite frankly, I need the distraction."

I quirk my head to the side. "From what?"

"From the fact that I lost the girl." He gives me a sad smile.

My mouth forms into an O when I decode his words. "Bent—"

"Naw, baby, don't do that. It's all good." He leans down and places a kiss on my cheek before taking a few steps backward. "I'll smoke a little more, drink a little more, and get lost in a pussy or three at the boathouse. I'll be just fine."

I'm still a little in shock from seeing this serious side of Bentley. I can't think of anything to say, so I just sit there like an idiot watching him walk away. A few minutes later, I'm still alone, getting more creeped out with each passing second. Why the hell Kingston thought leaving me in the woods by myself in the middle of the night was a good idea, I'll never know. That asshole better get here fast, or I'm walking back.

An owl hoots from somewhere above, adding to the ominous feeling in my gut. Where in the hell is he? I whip my head around when I hear a twig snapping behind me, followed by the crunching of shoes on the fallen leaves. *Fucking finally!*

I turn, expecting to see Kingston, but instead, I see two men wearing dark ski masks, coming right toward me. Oh, fuck.

I jump off the bench and immediately start running. Two masked dudes scream trouble. I'm not giving them a chance to bury my body out here. I can hear them behind me, but I'm not chancing looking back. I hate being so exposed, so I dart into the woods and pray the trees will provide some sort of camouflage.

"Oh, sweetheart, we like it when they run," a deep voice taunts behind me. "It makes catching our prey much more satisfying."

The other one laughs, the sound of their amusement chilling me to the bones. Who are these twisted fucks? And seriously, where the hell is Kingston? I almost trip in my flip-flops so I kick them off, running barefoot now. The sticks covering the forest floor scrape my skin, but I barely feel the pain because I'm too terrified to think of anything but escape.

"Help!" I scream. "Somebody fucking help me!"

I know we're far away from any houses, but I have to try getting someone's attention.

"We like it when they scream, too," the same man calls out. "But save your breath. There's no one out here to save you."

Shit. Fuck. Shit.

My eyes dart left and right, trying to decide which direction to go. I can feel them closing in on me, so I pump my legs harder and veer back toward the shore. Running straight along a path has to be better than going in circles. Just as I reach the mushy soil running along the water, I scream out in agony as I'm pulled back by my hair and slammed into the ground. My face is smashed into the mud as a heavy body covers mine from behind.

"Get off me!" I struggle as hard as I can, but he's so much bigger and heavier than me.

The asshole tightens his grip on my hair and pulls.

"Fucking hold still, bitch."

I try kneeing him in the balls as rough hands flip me over, but he predicts the move and blocks me.

"Fucking hold her feet!" the guy yells.

His partner grabs ahold of my ankles and secures me in place. The wind is knocked out of me as the other guy presses his knees to my chest and slams his meaty palm over my mouth. I see a flash of silver right before I feel the tip of a sharp blade at my throat.

"Now listen up, you cunt," he seethes. "This is how it's gonna go. You're going to stop trying to maim us and you're going to open those pretty legs of yours. If you try screaming for help again" —he presses the blade in farther— "I'll slit your fucking throat. If you take it like a good girl until we're done with you, you get to live. Understand?"

I fight against the panic brewing inside of me. I need to somehow keep a clear head and figure a way out of this.

Tears are pouring down my face as I nod my head as much as he'll allow.

The man removes the knife from my throat, trailing it between my breasts. "Are you going to be quiet if I remove my hand?"

I nod again.

I look up at the sky as the knife moves farther, focusing on the stars instead of the horror of my reality. I cry out when he grabs my breast roughly, pulling so hard it feels like he's trying to rip it off my body.

"Oh yeah, these are some real nice titties. Pretty little things, just like the rest of you. I wonder if they taste as good as they feel."

I whimper as I feel the cold blade against my shoulder before he cuts through one, then the other strap of my dress. He pushes the material out of the way and yanks my bra cups down, exposing my bare breasts. He rolls my nipples between his thumbs and forefingers before dipping his head and sucking one into his mouth. Bile rises in my throat but I hold it back, knowing if I vomited all over this guy, he'd be even rougher.

"Mmm, sweet as candy. I wonder how your pussy tastes." He bunches the lower half of my dress up.

I don't think I can take much more of this. I feel like I'm going to pass out.

"C'mon, man." The other guy stands up and starts pacing nervously. "This isn't what we're getting paid for."

What?! A scream curses inside my head when I feel the blade slicing through the strings on my panties. Asshole number one pulls the material away and leers down between my legs.

"Shut the fuck up," he says. "Do you see this gorgeous little pussy?" He runs the handle of the blade over my mound, slowly dragging it lower. "She's freshly waxed and everything. It's like she was waiting for us. Our employer will understand."

"Who's your employer?" I bite out. I figure if I'm

going to endure what's about to happen, I might as well get information so I can kill the fucker responsible for this afterward.

"Did I say you could talk?" Asshole One tsks.

The handle of the blade presses into my clit before going lower again, stopping at my entrance. Oh, God, this is really happening. I'm about to be raped with a knife in the middle of nowhere by some psycho. Violence rages inside of me, demanding I fight back, giving me the adrenaline spike I need to make it out of this relatively unharmed.

I buck my body, catching my attacker by surprise. The blade flies out of his hand onto the ground beside me.

"You're going to pay for that!" he screams right before punching me in the face.

Spots dance across my vision as I dive for the knife. I'm sure the alcohol and weed I've consumed tonight aren't helping. My attacker and I grapple while the other guy keeps pacing, mumbling something to himself.

I get to my feet as my fingers wrap around the handle, raising the knife threateningly. "Stay away from me! My boyfriend is going to be here any second, you prick!"

Kingston's not exactly my boyfriend, but that's not important right now. Asshole One distances himself, but he doesn't look nearly as bothered by the fact that I'm now wielding the weapon as he should be.

He gives me a smarmy smile. "Oh, you stupid, stupid girl. No one's coming for you. Who do you think led the lamb to the slaughter?" The guy laughs as he sees doubt creeping in. "That's right, sweetheart. Your precious boyfriend doesn't give a shit about you. Neither do his friends. Sweet talking you out of your panties was all part of the plan. Now, you're at our mercy."

My hand starts shaking. No, he's bluffing. He *has to be* bluffing. But why isn't Kingston here yet, I wonder?

"You're lying!" I scream, although there's no conviction behind my words.

He holds his arms out to his side. "Am I? You don't sound too sure."

My hand is shaking violently now. I scream when he lunges for me, tackling me back to the ground. He's twisting and squeezing my hand painfully, trying to get the knife but I refuse to let go. That is, until I hear a snap and excruciating pain forces me to release my grip.

He straddles me, raining blow after blow against my face. My eyes are filled with tears, making my vision blurry. One eye is so swollen, I can barely keep it open. The pain from my injuries are so intense, I'm drifting in and out of consciousness.

I keep fighting and screaming though, knowing it's my only hope. This man is too enraged and nothing is going to stop him unless he's incapacitated. I manage to land a solid blow to his nuts, causing him to bellow out in pain. The smile quickly dies on my bloodied and cracked lips when it feels like I'm being stabbed with a white-hot poker. Instinctively, I reach down with my broken hand and feel blood oozing out of my stomach.

My gaze locks on my attacker as I choke on the hot, metallic liquid rising up my throat. I turn my head, vomiting blood.

"Oh, shit, man!" the other guy yells. "You stabbed her! You fucking stabbed her! We need to get the hell out of here!"

The bastard stands up. "Look what you did, you dumb bitch. You could've just spread your legs and this would've never happened." He gives me a swift kick to the stomach to punctuate his statement before both men flee.

I double over, clutching my wound, trying to stay alert, but I'm not very successful at it. I'm not sure how long I lay there in my tattered dress. It could be minutes. It could be hours. My mind races as my battered body accepts its fate.

It's funny the things you think of when you're dying. Like, I wonder what kind of birthday cake Ainsley got? I was hoping for chocolate, maybe with a raspberry filling... although, I suppose it doesn't matter anymore. Or... it'd be really cool if I was walking on the beach right now, feeling the ocean tickle my toes as the waves crash against the shore. I bet some local going out for a jog will find my body. Haven't you ever noticed that? Runners always find the dead bodies. I can see the headlines now:

Teenager Stabbed to Death in Quaint, Mountain Town

It'll shake up this community temporarily, but before you know it, I'll just be that poor girl who died by the water's edge. Goosebumps scatter across my flesh as a chill courses through my body. Damn, it's cold up here. Of course, the one time I actually wear a dress, I get stuck out in the wilderness.

What really pisses me off—and yes, I have every right to be pissed as I lie here bleeding out—is that I can't stop thinking about the fact the people responsible for this will get away with it. They'll graduate high school, go off to college, eventually get married and pop out pretentious little babies, never looking back. Never knowing what it's like to have consequences for their actions. These people will always live in a world where you can solve any problem, get away with any vile act, by throwing a little money around.

My body sinks into the ground, the smell of mud and copper assaulting my senses. I really should get help, but moving isn't exactly an option. Screaming isn't one either—I've already tried that and all I have to show for it is a raw throat. My head lolls to the side, eyes falling to the glassy surface of the lake as the fingers on my non-broken hand flutter over my abdomen, unsuccessfully trying to staunch the flow of sticky blood.

As I stare unblinkingly at the full moon reflecting off the lake's surface, I realize the irony of my situation. I'm no stranger to violence—I've spent most of my life surrounded by it. When you're impoverished, or craving your next fix, you'd be surprised what people will do when desperation sinks in. That's why my mother taught me to be vigilant, to take precautions. I took her lessons to heart and managed to survive over seventeen years without incident.

It fucking figures that when I actually *do* become a victim of violence, it's in a place drenched in wealth.

I suppose that's what I get for trusting a liar.

The last thought I have before losing consciousness is that I'm going to make them pay. If I get out of this alive, I will make *every last one of them* pay for what they've done. And if I don't make it... if this is the end for me... I'll haunt those motherfuckers from the grave.

∽

To be continued in book two of the Windsor Academy series, RUTHLESS KINGS.

also available by laura lee

Dealing With Love Series (Interconnected standalones)

♥ Deal Breakers (Devyn & Riley's story)

♥ Deal Takers (Rainey & Brody's story)

♥ Deal Makers (Charlotte and Drew's story)

Bedding the Billionaire Series (Interconnected standalones)

♥ Billionaire Bosshole

♥ Billionaire Bossman (Formerly Public Relations)

♥ Billionaire Bad Boy (Formerly Sweet Temptations)

Windsor Academy Series (Books 1-3 must be read in order)

♥ Wicked Liars

♥ Ruthless Kings

♥ Fallen Heirs

♥ Broken Playboy (Bentley's story-can be read as a standalone)

Standalone Novels

♥Beautifully Broken

♥Happy New You

♥Redemption

GO TO: https://www.subscribepage.com/LauraLeeBooks to sign up for Laura's newsletter and you'll be the first to know when she has a sale or new release!

about the author

Laura Lee is the *USA Today* bestselling author of steamy and sometimes ridiculously funny romance. She won her first writing contest at the ripe old age of nine, earning a trip to the state capital to showcase her manuscript. Thankfully for her, those early works will never see the light of day again!

Laura lives in the Pacific Northwest with her wonderful husband, two beautiful children, and three of the most poorly behaved cats in existence. She likes her fruit smoothies filled with rum, her cupboards stocked with Cadbury's chocolate, and her music turned up loud. When she's not chasing the kids around, writing, or watching HGTV, she's reading anything she can get her hands on. She's a sucker for spicy romances, especially those that can make her laugh!

For more information about the author, check out her website at: www.LauraLeeBooks.com

You can also find her "working" on social media quite frequently.
Facebook: @LauraLeeBooks1
Instagram: @LauraLeeBooks
Twitter: @LauraLeeBooks
Verve Romance: @LauraLeeBooks
Reader's Group: Laura Lee's Lounge
TikTok: @AuthorLauraLee

acknowledgments

To my husband, Tad: You are my rock. Our world is in chaos right now and the one thing that never waivers is your love and support. I wouldn't want anyone else by my side in this crazy thing we call life.

To my beautiful children: You two breathe life into me. I love you more than anything.

To my friend and fellow author, Julia Wolf: Thank you for your brainstorming genius. This book wouldn't be out in the wild without you.

To my lovely beta, Crystal: Thank you for allowing me to pop your bully romance cherry. Your feedback, as always, was invaluable.

To all the seriously awesome bloggers & bookstagrammers in the book world: There's a lot of scary things going on in the world right now and we could all use a little escapism. Your tireless efforts to spread the love of reading romance helps with that. I appreciate you so much, as a reader and a writer.

To my incredible Feisty Fae, ARC team, and Loungers: Thank you for being such awesome, hilarious, wildly inappropriate, and supportive peeps. Do people even say peeps anymore?

To my editor, Ellie McLove of My Brother's Editor: Thank you for dealing with my delays and polishing my work to make the final product so much better! You're an absolute joy to work with.

Last but never least, to my readers: If you've been with me for a while, you know I like to write in several different romance subgenres. That said, this book is darker than anything I've written before. If you don't normally read bully romances but took a chance on it anyway, thank you for your faith in me. If you found me through this book, welcome to the craziness that is my brain! Whichever category you fall under, I appreciate you more than words can say. You are the reason I get to do what I love for a living.

Printed in Great Britain
by Amazon